Rudin

A Novel

Ivan Sergeevich Turgenev

(Translator: Constance Garnett)

Alpha Editions

This edition published in 2023

ISBN : 9789357930239

Design and Setting By
Alpha Editions
www.alphaedis.com
Email - info@alphaedis.com

Contents

INTRODUCTION

I

Turgenev is an author who no longer belongs to Russia only. During the last fifteen years of his life he won for himself the reading public, first in France, then in Germany and America, and finally in England.

In his funeral oration the spokesman of the most artistic and critical of European nations, Ernest Renan, hailed him as one of the greatest writers of our times: 'The Master, whose exquisite works have charmed our century, stands more than any other man as the incarnation of a whole race,' because 'a whole world lived in him and spoke through his mouth.' Not the Russian world only, we may add, but the whole Slavonic world, to which it was 'an honour to have been expressed by so great a Master.'

This recognition was, however, of slow growth. It had nothing in it of the sudden wave of curiosity and gushing enthusiasm which in a few years lifted Count Tolstoi to world-wide fame. Neither in the personality of Turgenev, nor in his talent, was there anything to strike and carry away popular imagination.

By the fecundity of his creative talent Turgenev stands with the greatest authors of all times. The gallery of living people, men, and especially women, each different and perfectly individualised, yet all the creatures of actual life, whom Turgenev introduces to us; the vast body of psychological truths he discovers, the subtle shades of men's feelings he reveals to us, is such as only the greatest among the great have succeeded in leaving as their artistic inheritance to their country and to the world.

As regards his method of dealing with his material and shaping it into mould, he stands even higher than as a pure creator. Tolstoi is more plastical, and certainly as deep and original and rich in creative power as Turgenev, and Dostoevsky is more intense, fervid, and dramatic. But as an *artist*, as master of the combination of details into a harmonious whole, as an architect of imaginative work, he surpasses all the prose writers of his country, and has but few equals among the great novelists of other lands. Twenty-five years ago, on reading the translation of one of his short stories (*Assya*), George Sand, who was then at the apogee of her fame, wrote to him: 'Master, all of us have to go to study at your school.' This was, indeed, a generous compliment, coming from the representative of French literature which is so eminently artistic. But it was not flattery. As an artist, Turgenev in reality stands with the classics who may be studied and admired for their perfect form long after the interest of their subject has disappeared. But it seems that in his very devotion to art and beauty he has purposely restricted the range of his creations.

To one familiar with all Turgenev's works it is evident that he possessed the keys of all human emotions, all human feelings, the highest and the lowest, the noble as well as the base. From the height of his superiority he saw all, understood all. Nature and men had no secrets hidden from his calm, penetrating eyes. In his latter days, sketches such as *Clara Militch*, *The Song of Triumphant Love*, *The Dream*, and the incomparable *Phantoms*, he showed that he could equal Edgar Poe, Hofmann, and Dostoevsky in the mastery of the fantastical, the horrible, the mysterious, and the incomprehensible, which live somewhere in human nerves, though not to be defined by reason.

But there was in him such a love of light, sunshine, and living human poetry, such an organic aversion for all that is ugly, or coarse and discordant, that he made himself almost exclusively the poet of the gentler side of human nature. On the fringe of his pictures or in their background, just for the sake of contrast, he will show us the vices, the cruelties, even the mire of life. But he cannot stay in these gloomy regions, and he hastens back to the realms of the sun and flowers, or to the poetical moonlight of melancholy, which he loves best because in it he can find expression for his own great sorrowing heart.

Even jealousy, which is the black shadow of the most poetical of human feelings, is avoided by the gentle artist. He hardly ever describes it, only alluding to it cursorily. But there is no novelist who gives so much room to the pure, crystalline, eternally youthful feeling of love. We may say that the description of love is Turgenev's speciality. What Francesco Petrarca did for one kind of love—the romantic, artificial, hot-house love of the times of chivalry—Turgenev did for the natural, spontaneous, modern love in all its variety of forms, kinds, and manifestations: the slow and gradual as well as the sudden and instantaneous; the spiritual, the admiring and inspiring, as well as the life-poisoning, terrible kind of love, which infects a man as a prolonged disease. There is something prodigious in Turgenev's insight into, and his inexhaustible richness, truthfulness, and freshness in the rendering of those emotions which have been the theme of all poets and novelists for two thousand years.

In the well-known memoirs of Caroline Bauer one comes across a curious legend about Paganini. She tells that the great enchanter owed his unique command over the emotions of his audiences to a peculiar use of one single string, G, which he made sing and whisper, cry and thunder, at the touch of his marvellous bow.

There is something of this in Turgenev's description of love. He has many other strings at his harp, but his greatest effect he obtains in touching this one. His stories are not love poems. He only prefers to present his people in the light of that feeling in which a man's soul gathers up all its highest energies, and melts as in a crucible, showing its dross and its pure metal.

Turgenev began his literary career and won an enormous popularity in Russia by his sketches from peasant life. His *Diary of a Sportsman* contains some of the best of his short stories, and his *Country Inn,* written a few years later, in the maturity of his talent, is as good as Tolstoi's little masterpiece, *Polikushka.*

He was certainly able to paint all classes and conditions of Russian people. But in his greater works Turgenev lays the action exclusively with one class of Russian people. There is nothing of the enormous canvas of Count Tolstoi, in which the whole of Russia seems to pass in review before the readers. In Turgenev's novels we see only educated Russia, or rather the more advanced thinking part of it, which he knew best, because he was a part of it himself.

We are far from regretting this specialisation. Quality can sometimes hold its own against quantity. Although small numerically, the section of Russian society which Turgenev represents is enormously interesting, because it is the brain of the nation, the living ferment which alone can leaven the huge unformed masses. It is upon them that depend the destinies of their country. Besides, the artistic value of his works could only be enhanced by his concentrating his genius upon a field so familiar to him, and engrossing so completely his mind and his sympathies. What he loses in dimensions he gains in correctness, depth, wonderful subtlety and effectiveness of every minute detail, and the surpassing beauty of the whole. The jewels of art he left us are like those which nations store in the sanctuaries of their museums and galleries to be admired, the longer they are studied. But we must look to Tolstoi for the huge and towering monuments, hewn in massive granite, to be put upon some cross way of nations as an object of wonder and admiration for all who come from the four winds of heaven.

Turgenev did not write for the masses but for the *elite* among men. The fact that he has won such a fame among foreigners, and that the number of his readers is widening every year, proves that great art is international, and also, I may say, that artistic taste and understanding is growing everywhere.

II

It is written that no man is a prophet in his own country, and from time immemorial all the unsuccessful aspirants to the profession have found their consolation in this proverbial truth. But for aught we know this hard limitation has never been applied to artists. Indeed it seems absurd on the face of it that the artist's countrymen, for whom and about whom he writes, should be less fit to recognise him than strangers. Yet in certain special and peculiar conditions, the most unlikely things will sometimes occur, as is proved in the case of Turgenev.

The fact is that *as an artist* he was appreciated to his full value first by foreigners. The Russians have begun to understand him, and to assign to him his right place in this respect only now, after his death, whilst in his lifetime his *artistic genius* was comparatively little cared for, save by a handful of his personal friends.

This supreme art told upon the Russian public unconsciously, as it was bound to tell upon a nation so richly endowed with natural artistic instinct. Turgenev was always the most widely read of Russian authors, not excepting Tolstoi, who came to the front only after his death. But full recognition he had not, because he happened to produce his works in a troubled epoch of political and social strife, when the best men were absorbed in other interests and pursuits, and could not and would not appreciate and enjoy pure art. This was the painful, almost tragic, position of an artist, who lived in a most inartistic epoch, and whose highest aspirations and noblest efforts wounded and irritated those among his countrymen whom he was most devoted to, and whom he desired most ardently to serve.

This strife embittered Turgenev's life.

At one crucial epoch of his literary career the conflict became so vehement, and the outcry against him, set in motion by his very artistic truthfulness and objectiveness, became so loud and unanimous, that he contemplated giving up literature altogether. He could not possibly have held to this resolution. But it is surely an open question whether, sensitive and modest as he was, and prone to despondency and diffidence, he would have done so much for the literature of his country without the enthusiastic encouragement of various great foreign novelists, who were his friends and admirers: George Sand, Gustave Flaubert, in France; Auerbach, in Germany; W. D. Howells, in America; George Eliot, in England.

We will tell the story of his troubled life piece by piece as far as space will allow, as his works appear in succession. Here we will only give a few biographical traits which bear particularly upon the novel before us, and account for his peculiar hold over the minds of his countrymen.

Turgenev, who was born in 1818, belonged to a set of Russians very small in his time, who had received a thoroughly European education in no way inferior to that of the best favoured young German or Englishman. It happened, moreover, that his paternal uncle, Nicholas Turgenev, the famous 'Decembrist,' after the failure of that first attempt (December 14, 1825) to gain by force of arms a constitutional government for Russia, succeeded in escaping the vengeance of the Tsar Nicholas I., and settled in France, where he published in French the first vindication of Russian revolution.

Whilst studying philosophy in the Berlin University, Turgenev paid short visits to his uncle, who initiated him in the ideas of liberty, from which he never swerved throughout his long life.

In the sixties, when Alexander Hertzen, one of the most gifted writers of our land, a sparkling, witty, pathetic, and powerful journalist and brilliant essayist, started in London his *Kolokol*, a revolutionary, or rather radical paper, which had a great influence in Russia, Turgenev became one of his most active contributors and advisers,—almost a member of the editorial staff.

This fact has been revealed a few years ago by the publication, which we owe to Professor Dragomanov, of the private correspondence between Turgenev and Hertzen. This most interesting little volume throws quite a new light upon Turgenev, showing that our great novelist was at the same time one of the strongest—perhaps the strongest—and most clear-sighted political thinkers of his time. However surprising such a versatility may appear, it is proved to demonstration by a comparison of his views, his attitude, and his forecasts, some of which have been verified only lately, with those of the acknowledged leaders and spokesmen of the various political parties of his day, including Alexander Hertzen himself. Turgenev's are always the soundest, the most correct and far-sighted judgments, as latter-day history has proved.

A man with so ardent a love of liberty, and such radical views, could not possibly banish them from his literary works, no matter how great his devotion to pure art. He would have been a poor artist had he inflicted upon himself such a mutilation, because freedom from all restraints, the frank, sincere expression of the artist's individuality, is the life and soul of all true art.

Turgenev gave to his country the whole of himself, the best of his mind and of his creative fancy. He appeared at the same time as a teacher, a prophet of new ideas, and as a poet and artist. But his own countrymen hailed him in the first capacity, remaining for a long time obtuse to the latter and greater.

Thus, during one of the most important and interesting periods of our national history, Turgenev was the standard-bearer and inspirer of the Liberal, the thinking Russia. Although the two men stand at diametrically opposite poles, Turgenev's position can be compared to that of Count Tolstoi nowadays, with a difference, this time in favour of the author of *Dmitri Rudin*. With Turgenev the thinker and the artist are not at war, spoiling and sometimes contradicting each other's efforts. They go hand in hand, because he never preaches any doctrine whatever, but gives us, with an unimpeachable, artistic objectiveness, the living men and women in whom certain ideas, doctrines, and aspirations were embodied. And he never evolves these ideas and doctrines from his inner consciousness, but takes them from real life, catching with his unfailing artistic instinct an incipient movement just at the moment when it was to become a historic feature of the time. Thus his novels are a sort of artistic epitome of the intellectual history of modern Russia, and also a powerful instrument of her intellectual progress.

III

Rudin is the first of Turgenev's social novels, and is a sort of artistic introduction to those that follow, because it refers to the epoch anterior to that when the present social and political movements began. This epoch is being fast forgotten, and without his novel it would be difficult for us to fully realise it, but it is well worth studying, because we find in it the germ of future growths.

It was a gloomy time. The ferocious despotism of Nicholas I.—overweighing the country like the stone lid of a coffin, crushed every word, every thought, which did not fit with its narrow conceptions. But this was not the worst. The worst was that progressive Russia was represented by a mere handful of men, who were so immensely in advance of their surroundings, that in their own country they felt more isolated, helpless, and out of touch with the realities of life than if they had lived among strangers.

But men must have some outlet for their spiritual energies, and these men, unable to take part in the sordid or petty pursuits of those around them, created for themselves artificial life, artificial pursuits and interests.

The isolation in which they lived drew them naturally together. The 'circle,' something between an informal club and a debating society, became the form in which these cravings of mind or heart could be satisfied. These people met and talked; that was all they were able to do.

The passage in which one of the heroes, Lezhnyov, tells the woman he loves about the circle of which Dmitri Rudin and himself were members, is historically one of the most suggestive. It refers to a circle of young students. But it has a wider application. All prominent men of the epoch—Stankevitch, who served as model to the poetic and touching figure of Pokorsky; Alexander Hertzen, and the great critic, Belinsky—all had their 'circles,' or their small chapels, in which these enthusiasts met to offer worship to the 'goddess of truth, art, and morality.'

They were the best men of their time, full of high aspirations and knowledge, and their disinterested search after truth was certainly a noble pursuit. They had full right to look down upon their neighbours wallowing in the mire of sordid and selfish materialism. But by living in that spiritual hothouse of dreams, philosophical speculations, and abstractions, these men unfitted themselves only the more completely for participation in real life; the absorption in interests having nothing to do with the life of their own country, estranged them still more from it. The overwhelming stream of words drained them of the natural sources of spontaneous emotion, and these men almost grew out of feeling by dint of constantly analysing their feelings.

Dmitri Rudin is the typical man of that generation, both the victim and the hero of his time—a man who is almost a Titan in word and a pigmy in deed. He is eloquent as a young Demosthenes. An irresistible debater, he carries everything before him the moment he appears. But he fails ignominiously when put to the hard test of action. Yet he is not an impostor. His enthusiasm is contagious because it is sincere, and his eloquence is convincing because devotion to his ideals is an absorbing passion with him. He would die for them, and, what is more rare, he would not swerve a hair's-breadth from them for any worldly advantage, or for fear of any hardship. Only this passion and this enthusiasm spring with him entirely from the head. The heart, the deep emotional power of human love and pity, lay dormant in him. Humanity, which he would serve to the last drop of his blood, is for him a body of foreigners—French, English, Germans—whom he has studied from books, and whom he has met only in hotels and watering-places during his foreign travels as a student or as a tourist.

Towards such an abstract, alien humanity, a man cannot feel any real attachment. With all his outward ardour, Rudin is cold as ice at the bottom of his heart. His is an enthusiasm which glows without warmth, like the aurora borealis of the Polar regions. A poor substitute for the bountiful sun. But what would have become of a God-forsaken land if the Arctic nights were deprived of that substitute? With all their weaknesses, Rudin and the men of his stamp—in other words, the men of the generation of 1840—have rendered an heroic service to their country. They inculcated in it the religion of the ideal; they brought in the seeds, which had only to be thrown into the warm furrow of their native soil to bring forth the rich crops of the future.

The shortcomings and the impotence of these men were due to their having no organic ties with their own country, no roots in the Russian soil. They hardly knew the Russian people, who appeared to them as nothing more than an historic abstraction. They were really cosmopolitan, as a poor makeshift for something better, and Turgenev, in making his hero die on a French barricade, was true to life as well as to art.

The inward growth of the country has remedied this defect in the course of the three generations which have followed. But has the remedy been complete? No; far from it, unfortunately. There are still thousands of barriers preventing the Russians from doing something useful for their countrymen and mixing freely with them. The spiritual energies of the most ardent are still compelled—partially at least—to run into the artificial channels described in Turgenev's novel.

Hence the perpetuation of Rudin's type, which acquires more than an historical interest.

In discussing the character of Hlestakov, the hero of his great comedy, Gogol declared that this type is pretty nigh universal, because 'every Russian,' he says, 'has a bit of Hlestakov in him.' This not very flattering opinion has been humbly indorsed and repeated since, out of reverence to Gogol's great authority, although it is untrue on the face of it. Hlestakov is a sort of Tartarin in Russian dress, whilst simplicity and sincerity are the fundamental traits of all that is Russian in character, manner, art, literature. But it may be truly said that every educated Russian of our time has a bit of Dmitri Rudin in him.

This figure is undoubtedly one of the finest in Turgenev's gallery, and it is at the same time one of the most brilliant examples of his artistic method.

Turgenev does not give us at one stroke sculptured figures made from one block, such as rise before us from Tolstoi's pages. His art is rather that of a painter or musical composer than of a sculptor. He has more colour, a deeper perspective, a greater variety of lights and shadows—a more complete portraiture of the spiritual man. Tolstoi's people stand so living and concrete that one feels one can recognise them in the street. Turgenev's are like people whose intimate confessions and private correspondence, unveiling all the secrets of their spiritual life, have been submitted to one.

Every scene, almost every line, opens up new deep horizons, throwing upon his people some new unexpected light.

The extremely complex and difficult character of the hero of this story, shows at its highest this subtle psychological many-sidedness. Dmitri Rudin is built up of contradictions, yet not for a moment does he cease to be perfectly real, living, and concrete.

Hardly less remarkable is the character of the heroine, Natalya, the quiet, sober, matter-of-fact girl, who at the bottom is an enthusiastic and heroic nature. She is but a child fresh to all impressions of life, and as yet undeveloped. To have used the searching, analytical method in painting her would have spoiled this beautiful creation. Turgenev describes her synthetically by a few masterly lines, which show us, however, the secrets of her spirit; revealing what she is and also what she might have become under other circumstances.

This character deserves more attention than we can give it here. Turgenev, like George Meredith, is a master in painting women, and his Natalya is the first poetical revelation of a very striking fact in modern Russian history; the appearance of women possessing a strength of mind more finely masculine than that of the men of their time. By the side of weak, irresolute, though highly intellectual men we see in his first three novels energetic, earnest, impassioned women, who take the lead in action, whilst they are but the man's modest pupils in the domain of ideas. Only later on, in *Fathers and Children*, does Turgenev show us in Bazarov a man essentially masculine. But of this interesting peculiarity of Russian intellectual life, in the years 1840 to 1860, I will speak more fully when analysing another of Turgenev's novels in which this contrast is most conspicuous.

I will say nothing of the minor characters of the story before us: Lezhnyov, Pigasov, Madame Lasunsky, Pandalevsky, who are all excellent examples of what may be called miniature-painting.

As to the novel as a whole, I will make here only one observation, not to forestall the reader's own impressions.

Turgenev is a realist in the sense that he keeps close to reality, truth, and nature. But in the pursuit of photographic faithfulness to life, he never allows himself to be tedious and dull, as some of the best representatives of the school think it incumbent upon them to be. His descriptions are never overburdened with wearisome details; his action is rapid; the events are never to be foreseen a hundred pages beforehand; he keeps his readers in constant suspense. And it seems to me in so doing he shows himself a better realist than the gifted representatives of the orthodox realism in France, England, and America. Life is not dull; life is full of the unforeseen, full of suspense. A novelist, however natural and logical, must contrive to have it in his novels if he is not to sacrifice the soul of art for the merest show of fidelity.

The plot of Dmitri Rudin is so exceedingly simple that an English novel-reader would say that there is hardly any plot at all. Turgenev disdained the tricks of the sensational novelists. Yet, for a Russian at least, it is easier to lay down before the end a novel by Victor Hugo or Alexander Dumas than Dmitri Rudin, or, indeed, any of Turgenev's great novels. What the novelists of the romantic school obtain by the charm of unexpected adventures and thrilling situations, Turgenev succeeds in obtaining by the brisk admirably concentrated action, and, above all, by the simplest and most precious of a novelist's gifts: his unique command over the sympathies and emotions of his readers. In this he can be compared to a musician who works upon the nerves and the souls of his audience without the intermediary of the mind;

or, better still, to a poet who combines the power of the word with the magic spell of harmony. One does not read his novels; one lives in them.

Much of this peculiar gift of fascination is certainly due to Turgenev's mastery over all the resources of our rich, flexible, and musical language. The poet Lermontov alone wrote as splendid a prose as Turgenev. A good deal of its charm is unavoidably lost in translation. But I am happy to say that the present one is as near an approach to the elegance and poetry of the original as I have ever come across.

S. STEPNIAK.

BEDFORD PARK, April 20, 1894.

THE NAMES OF THE CHARACTERS IN THE BOOK

DMITRI NIKOLA'ITCH RU'DIN.
DAR-YA MIHA'ILOVNA LASU'NSKY.
NATA'L-YA ALEX-YE'VNA.
MIHA'ILO MIHA'ILITCH LE'ZH-NYOV (MISHA).
ALEXANDRA PA'VLOVNA LI'PIN (SASHA).
SERGEI (pron, Sergay) PA'VLITCH VOLI'NT-SEV (SEREZHA).
KONSTANTIN DIOMIDITCH PANDALE'VSKY.
AFRICAN SEME'NITCH PIGA'SOV.
BASSI'STOFF.
MLLE. BONCOURT.

I

IT was a quiet summer morning. The sun stood already pretty high in the clear sky but the fields were still sparkling with dew; a fresh breeze blew fragrantly from the scarce awakened valleys and in the forest, still damp and hushed, the birds were merrily carolling their morning song. On the ridge of a swelling upland, which was covered from base to summit with blossoming rye, a little village was to be seen. Along a narrow by-road to this little village a young woman was walking in a white muslin gown, and a round straw, hat, with a parasol in her hand. A page boy followed her some distance behind.

She moved without haste and as though she were enjoying the walk. The high nodding rye all round her moved in long softly rustling waves, taking here a shade of silvery green and there a ripple of red; the larks were trilling overhead. The young woman had come from her own estate, which was not more than a mile from the village to which she was turning her steps. Her name was Alexandra Pavlovna Lipin. She was a widow, childless, and fairly well off, and lived with her brother, a retired cavalry officer, Sergei Pavlitch Volintsev. He was unmarried and looked after her property.

Alexandra Pavlovna reached the village and, stopping at the last hut, a very old and low one, she called up the boy and told him to go in and ask after the health of its mistress. He quickly came back accompanied by a decrepit old peasant with a white beard.

'Well, how is she?' asked Alexandra Pavlovna.

'Well, she is still alive,' began the old man.

'Can I go in?'

'Of course; yes.'

Alexandra Pavlovna went into the hut. It was narrow, stifling, and smoky inside. Some one stirred and began to moan on the stove which formed the bed. Alexandra Pavlovna looked round and discerned in the half darkness the yellow wrinkled face of the old woman tied up in a checked handkerchief. Covered to the very throat with a heavy overcoat she was breathing with difficulty, and her wasted hands were twitching.

Alexandra Pavlovna went close up to the old woman and laid her fingers on her forehead; it was burning hot.

'How do you feel, Matrona?' she inquired, bending over the bed.

'Oh, oh!' groaned the old woman, trying to make her out, 'bad, very bad, my dear! My last hour has come, my darling!'

'God is merciful, Matrona; perhaps you will be better soon. Did you take the medicine I sent you?'

The old woman groaned painfully, and did not answer. She had hardly heard the question.

'She has taken it,' said the old man who was standing at the door.

Alexandra Pavlovna turned to him.

'Is there no one with her but you?' she inquired.

'There is the girl—her granddaughter, but she always keeps away. She won't sit with her; she's such a gad-about. To give the old woman a drink of water is too much trouble for her. And I am old; what use can I be?'

'Shouldn't she be taken to me—to the hospital?'

'No. Why take her to the hospital? She would die just the same. She has lived her life; it's God's will now seemingly. She will never get up again. How could she go to the hospital? If they tried to lift her up, she would die.'

'Oh!' moaned the sick woman, 'my pretty lady, don't abandon my little orphan; our master is far away, but you——'

She could not go on, she had spent all her strength in saying so much.

'Do not worry yourself,' replied Alexandra Pavlovna, 'everything shall be done. Here is some tea and sugar I have brought you. If you can fancy it you must drink some. Have you a samovar, I wonder?' she added, looking at the old man.

'A samovar? We haven't a samovar, but we could get one.'

'Then get one, or I will send you one. And tell your granddaughter not to leave her like this. Tell her it's shameful.'

The old man made no answer but took the parcel of tea and sugar with both hands.

'Well, good-bye, Matrona!' said Alexandra Pavlovna, 'I will come and see you again; and you must not lose heart but take your medicine regularly.'

The old woman raised her head and drew herself a little towards Alexandra Pavlovna.

'Give me your little hand, dear lady,' she muttered.

Alexandra Pavlovna did not give her hand; she bent over her and kissed her on the forehead.

'Take care, now,' she said to the old man as she went out, 'and give her the medicine without fail, as it is written down, and give her some tea to drink.'

Again the old man made no reply, but only bowed.

Alexandra Pavlovna breathed more freely when she came out into the fresh air. She put up her parasol and was about to start homewards, when suddenly there appeared round the corner of a little hut a man about thirty, driving a low racing droshky and wearing an old overcoat of grey linen, and a foraging cap of the same. Catching sight of Alexandra Pavlovna he at once stopped his horse and turned round towards her. His broad and colourless face with its small light grey eyes and almost white moustache seemed all in the same tone of colour as his clothes.

'Good-morning!' he began, with a lazy smile; 'what are you doing here, if I may ask?'

'I have been visiting a sick woman... And where have you come from, Mihailo Mihailitch?'

The man addressed as Mihailo Mihailitch looked into her eyes and smiled again.

'You do well,' he said, 'to visit the sick, but wouldn't it be better for you to take her into the hospital?'

'She is too weak; impossible to move her.'

'But don't you intend to give up your hospital?'

'Give it up? Why?'

'Oh, I thought so.'

'What a strange notion! What put such an idea into your head?'

'Oh, you are always with Madame Lasunsky now, you know, and seem to be under her influence. And in her words—hospitals, schools, and all that sort of things, are mere waste of time—useless fads. Philanthropy ought to be entirely personal, and education too, all that is the soul's work... that's how she expresses herself, I believe. From whom did she pick up that opinion I should like to know?'

Alexandra Pavlovna laughed.

'Darya Mihailovna is a clever woman, I like and esteem her very much; but she may make mistakes, and I don't put faith in everything she says.'

'And it's a very good thing you don't,' rejoined Mihailo Mihailitch, who all the while remained sitting in his droshky, 'for she doesn't put much faith in what she says herself. I'm very glad I met you.'

'Why?'

'That's a nice question! As though it wasn't always delightful to meet you? To-day you look as bright and fresh as this morning.'

Alexandra Pavlovna laughed again.

'What are you laughing at?'

'What, indeed! If you could see with what a cold and indifferent face you brought out your compliment! I wonder you didn't yawn over the last word!'

'A cold face.... You always want fire; but fire is of no use at all. It flares and smokes and goes out.'

'And warms,'... put in Alexandra Pavlovna.

'Yes... and burns.'

'Well, what if it does burn! That's no great harm either! It's better anyway than——'

'Well, we shall see what you will say when you do get nicely burnt one day,' Mihailo Mihailitch interrupted her in a tone of vexation and made a cut at the horse with the reins, 'Good-bye.'

'Mihailo Mihailitch, stop a minute!' cried Alexandra Pavlovna, 'when are you coming to see us?'

'To-morrow; my greetings to your brother.'

And the droshky rolled away.

Alexandra Pavlovna looked after Mihailo Mihailitch.

'What a sack!' she thought. Sitting huddled up and covered with dust, his cap on the back of his head and tufts of flaxen hair straggling from beneath it, he looked strikingly like a huge sack of flour.

Alexandra Pavlovna turned tranquilly back along the path homewards. She was walking with downcast eyes. The tramp of a horse near made her stop and raise her head.... Her brother had come on horseback to meet her; beside him was walking a young man of medium height, wearing a light open coat, a light tie, and a light grey hat, and carrying a cane in his hand. He had been smiling for a long time at Alexandra Pavlovna, even though he saw that she was absorbed in thought and noticing nothing, and when she stopped he went up to her and in a tone of delight, almost of emotion, cried:

'Good-morning, Alexandra Pavlovna, good-morning!'

'Ah! Konstantin Diomiditch! good-morning!' she replied. 'You have come from Darya Mihailovna?'

'Precisely so, precisely so,' rejoined the young man with a radiant face, 'from Darya Mihailovna. Darya Mihailovna sent me to you; I preferred to walk.... It's such a glorious morning, and the distance is only three miles. When I arrived, you were not at home. Your brother told me you had gone to Semenovka; and he was just going out to the fields; so you see I walked with him to meet you. Yes, yes. How very delightful!'

The young man spoke Russian accurately and grammatically but with a foreign accent, though it was difficult to determine exactly what accent it was. In his features there was something Asiatic. His long hook nose, his large expressionless prominent eyes, his thick red lips, and retreating forehead, and his jet black hair,—everything about him suggested an Oriental extraction; but the young man gave his surname as Pandalevsky and spoke of Odessa as his birthplace, though he was brought up somewhere in White Russia at the expense of a rich and benevolent widow.

Another widow had obtained a government post for him. Middle-aged ladies were generally ready to befriend Konstantin Diomiditch; he knew well how to court them and was successful in coming across them. He was at this very time living with a rich lady, a landowner, Darya Mihailovna Lasunsky, in a position between that of a guest and of a dependant. He was very polite and obliging, full of sensibility and secretly given to sensuality, he had a pleasant voice, played well on the piano, and had the habit of gazing intently into the eyes of any one he was speaking to. He dressed very neatly, and wore his clothes a very long time, shaved his broad chin carefully, and arranged his hair curl by curl.

Alexandra Pavlovna heard his speech to the end and turned to her brother.

'I keep meeting people to-day; I have just been talking to Lezhnyov.'

'Oh, Lezhnyov! was he driving somewhere?'

'Yes, and fancy; he was in a racing droshky, and dressed in a kind of linen sack, all covered with dust.... What a queer creature he is!'

'Perhaps so; but he's a capital fellow.'

'Who? Mr. Lezhnyov?' inquired Pandalevsky, as though he were surprised.

'Yes, Mihailo Mihailitch Lezhnyov,' replied Volintsev. 'Well, good-bye; it's time I was off to the field; they are sowing your buckwheat. Mr. Pandalevsky will escort you home.' And Volintsev rode off at a trot.

'With the greatest of pleasure!' cried Konstantin Diomiditch, offering Alexandra Pavlovna his arm.

She took it and they both turned along the path to her house.

Walking with Alexandra Pavlovna on his arm seemed to afford Konstantin Diomiditch great delight; he moved with little steps, smiling, and his Oriental eyes were even be-dimmed by a slight moisture, though this indeed was no rare occurrence with them; it did not mean much for Konstantin Diomiditch to be moved and dissolve into tears. And who would not have been pleased to have on his arm a pretty, young and graceful woman? Of Alexandra Pavlovna the whole of her district was unanimous in declaring that she was charming, and the district was not wrong. Her straight, ever so slightly tilted nose would have been enough alone to drive any man out of his senses, to say nothing of her velvety dark eyes, her golden brown hair, the dimples in her smoothly curved cheeks, and her other beauties. But best of all was the sweet expression of her face; confiding, good and gentle, it touched and attracted at the same time. Alexandra Pavlovna had the glance and the smile of a child; other ladies found her a little simple.... Could one wish for anything more?

'Darya Mihailovna sent you to me, did you say?' she asked Pandalevsky.

'Yes; she sent me,' he answered, pronouncing the letter *s* like the English *th*. 'She particularly wishes and told me to beg you very urgently to be so good as to dine with her to-day. She is expecting a new guest whom she particularly wishes you to meet.'

'Who is it?'

'A certain Muffel, a baron, a gentleman of the bed-chamber from Petersburg. Darya Mihailovna made his acquaintance lately at the Prince Garin's, and speaks of him in high terms as an agreeable and cultivated young man. His Excellency the baron is interested, too, in literature, or more strictly speaking——ah! what an exquisite butterfly! pray look at it!——more strictly speaking, in political economy. He has written an essay on some very interesting question, and wants to submit it to Darya Mihailovna's criticism.'

'An article on political economy?'

'From the literary point of view, Alexandra Pavlovna, from the literary point of view. You are well aware, I suppose, that in that line Darya Mihailovna is an authority. Zhukovsky used to ask her advice, and my benefactor, who lives at Odessa, that benevolent old man, Roxolan Mediarovitch Ksandrika—— No doubt you know the name of that eminent man?'

'No; I have never heard of him.'

'You never heard of such a man? surprising! I was going to say that Roxolan Mediarovitch always had the very highest opinion of Darya Mihailovna's knowledge of Russian!

'Is this baron a pedant then?' asked Alexandra Pavlovna.

'Not in the very least. Darya Mihailovna says, on the contrary, that you see that he belongs to the best society at once. He spoke of Beethoven with such eloquence that even the old prince was quite delighted by it. That, I own, I should like to have heard; you know that is in my line. Allow me to offer you this lovely wild-flower.'

Alexandra Pavlovna took the flower, and when she had walked a few steps farther, let it drop on the path. They were not more than two hundred paces from her house. It had been recently built and whitewashed, and looked out hospitably with its wide light windows from the thick foliage of the old limes and maples.

'So what message do you give me for Darya Mihailovna?' began Pandalevsky, slightly hurt at the fate of the flower he had given her. 'Will you come to dinner? She invites your brother too.'

'Yes; we will come, most certainly. And how is Natasha?'

'Natalya Alexyevna is well, I am glad to say. But we have already passed the road that turns off to Darya Mihailovna's. Allow me to bid you good-bye.'

Alexandra Pavlovna stopped. 'But won't you come in?' she said in a hesitating voice.

'I should like to, indeed, but I am afraid it is late. Darya Mihailovna wishes to hear a new étude of Thalberg's, so I must practise and have it ready. Besides, I am doubtful, I must confess, whether my visit could afford you any pleasure.'

'Oh, no! why?'

Pandalevsky sighed and dropped his eyes expressively.

'Good-bye, Alexandra Pavlovna!' he said after a slight pause; then he bowed and turned back.

Alexandra Pavlovna turned round and went home.

Konstantin Diomiditch, too, walked homewards. All softness had vanished at once from his face; a self-confident, almost hard expression came into it. Even his walk was changed; his steps were longer and he trod more heavily. He had walked about two miles, carelessly swinging his cane, when all at once he began to smile again: he saw by the roadside a young, rather pretty peasant girl, who was driving some calves out of an oat-field. Konstantin Diomiditch approached the girl as warily as a cat, and began to speak to her. She said nothing at first, only blushed and laughed, but at last she hid her face in her sleeve, turned away, and muttered:

'Go away, sir; upon my word...'

Konstantin Diomiditch shook his finger at her and told her to bring him some cornflowers.

'What do you want with cornflowers?—to make a wreath?' replied the girl; 'come now, go along then.'

'Stop a minute, my pretty little dear,' Konstantin Diomiditch was beginning.

'There now, go along,' the girl interrupted him, 'there are the young gentlemen coming.'

Konstantin Diomiditch looked round. There really were Vanya and Petya, Darya Mihailovna's sons, running along the road; after them walked their tutor, Bassistoff, a young man of two-and-twenty, who had only just left college. Bassistoff was a well-grown youth, with a simple face, a large nose, thick lips, and small pig's eyes, plain and awkward, but kind, good, and upright. He dressed untidily and wore his hair long—not from affectation, but from laziness; he liked eating and he liked sleeping, but he also liked a good book, and an earnest conversation, and he hated Pandalevsky from the depths of his soul.

Darya Mihailovna's children worshipped Bassistoff, and yet were not in the least afraid of him; he was on a friendly footing with all the rest of the household, a fact which was not altogether pleasing to its mistress, though she was fond of declaring that for her social prejudices did not exist.

'Good-morning, my dears,' began Konstantin Diomiditch, 'how early you have come for your walk to-day! But I,' he added, turning to Bassistoff, 'have been out a long while already; it's my passion—to enjoy nature.'

'We saw how you were enjoying nature,' muttered Bassistoff.

'You are a materialist, God knows what you are imagining! I know you.' When Pandalevsky spoke to Bassistoff or people like him, he grew slightly irritated, and pronounced the letter *s* quite clearly, even with a slight hiss.

'Why, were you asking your way of that girl, am I to suppose?' said Bassistoff, shifting his eyes to right and to left.

He felt that Pandalevsky was looking him straight in the face, and this fact was exceedingly unpleasant to him. 'I repeat, a materialist and nothing more.'

'You certainly prefer to see only the prosaic side in everything.'

'Boys!' cried Bassistoff suddenly, 'do you see that willow at the corner? let's see who can get to it first. One! two! three! and away!'

The boys set off at full speed to the willow. Bassistoff rushed after them.

'What a lout!' thought Pandalevsky, 'he is spoiling those boys. A perfect peasant!'

And looking with satisfaction at his own neat and elegant figure, Konstantin Diomiditch struck his coat-sleeve twice with his open hand, pulled up his collar, and went on his way. When he had reached his own room, he put on an old dressing-gown and sat down with an anxious face to the piano.

II

Darya Mihailovna's house was regarded as almost the first in the whole province. It was a huge stone mansion, built after designs of Rastrelli in the taste of last century, and in a commanding position on the summit of a hill, at whose base flowed one of the principal rivers of central Russia. Darya Mihailovna herself was a wealthy and distinguished lady, the widow of a privy councillor. Pandalevsky said of her, that she knew all Europe and all Europe knew her! However, Europe knew her very little; even at Petersburg she had not played a very prominent part; but on the other hand at Moscow every one knew her and visited her. She belonged to the highest society, and was spoken of as a rather eccentric woman, not wholly good-natured, but excessively clever. In her youth she had been very pretty. Poets had written verses to her, young men had been in love with her, distinguished men had paid her homage. But twenty-five or thirty years had passed since those days and not a trace of her former charms remained. Every one who saw her now for the first time was impelled to ask himself, if this woman—skinny, sharp-nosed, and yellow-faced, though still not old in years—could once have been a beauty, if she was really the same woman who had been the inspiration of poets.... And every one marvelled inwardly at the mutability of earthly things. It is true that Pandalevsky discovered that Darya Mihailovna had preserved her magnificent eyes in a marvellous way; but we have seen that Pandalevsky also maintained that all Europe knew her.

Darya Mihailovna went every summer to her country place with her children (she had three: a daughter of seventeen, Natalya, and two sons of nine and ten years old). She kept open house in the country, that is, she received men, especially unmarried ones; provincial ladies she could not endure. But what of the treatment she received from those ladies in return?

Darya Mihailovna, according to them, was a haughty, immoral, and insufferable tyrant, and above all—she permitted herself such liberties in conversation, it was shocking! Darya Mihailovna certainly did not care to stand on ceremony in the country, and in the unconstrained frankness of her manners there was perceptible a slight shade of the contempt of the lioness of the capital for the petty and obscure creatures who surrounded her. She had a careless, and even a sarcastic manner with her own set; but the shade of contempt was not there.

By the way, reader, have you observed that a person who is exceptionally nonchalant with his inferiors, is never nonchalant with persons of a higher rank? Why is that? But such questions lead to nothing.

When Konstantin Diomiditch, having at last learnt by heart the *étude* of Thalberg, went down from his bright and cheerful room to the drawing-room, he already found the whole household assembled. The salon was already beginning. The lady of the house was reposing on a wide couch, her feet gathered up under her, and a new French pamphlet in her hand; at the window behind a tambour frame, sat on one side the daughter of Darya Mihailovna, on the other, Mlle. Boncourt, the governess, a dry old maiden lady of sixty, with a false front of black curls under a parti-coloured cap and cotton wool in her ears; in the corner near the door was huddled Bassistoff reading a paper, near him were Petya and Vanya playing draughts, and leaning by the stove, his hands clasped behind his back, was a gentleman of low stature, with a swarthy face covered with bristling grey hair, and fiery black eyes—a certain African Semenitch Pigasov.

This Pigasov was a strange person. Full of acerbity against everything and every one—especially against women—he was railing from morning to night, sometimes very aptly, sometimes rather stupidly, but always with gusto. His ill-humour almost approached puerility; his laugh, the sound of his voice, his whole being seemed steeped in venom. Darya Mihailovna gave Pigasov a cordial reception; he amused her with his sallies. They were certainly absurd enough. He took delight in perpetual exaggeration. For example, if he were told of any disaster, that a village had been struck by lightning, or that a mill had been carried away by floods, or that a peasant had cut his hand with an axe, he invariably asked with concentrated bitterness, 'And what's her name?' meaning, what is the name of the woman responsible for this calamity, for according to his convictions, a woman was the cause of every misfortune, if you only looked deep enough into the matter. He once threw himself on his knees before a lady he hardly knew at all, who had been effusive in her hospitality to him and began tearfully, but with wrath written on his face, to entreat her to have compassion on him, saying that he had done her no harm and never would come to see her for the future. Once a horse had bolted with one of Darya Mihailovna's maids, thrown her into a ditch and almost killed her. From that time Pigasov never spoke of that horse except as the 'good, good horse,' and he even came to regard the hill and the ditch as specially picturesque spots. Pigasov had failed in life and had adopted this whimsical craze. He came of poor parents. His father had filled various petty posts, and could scarcely read and write, and did not trouble himself about his son's education; he fed and clothed him and nothing more. His mother spoiled him, but she died early. Pigasov educated himself, sent himself to the district school and then to the gymnasium, taught himself French, German, and even Latin, and, leaving the gymnasiums with an excellent certificate, went to Dorpat, where he maintained a perpetual struggle with poverty, but succeeded in completing his three years' course. Pigasov's abilities did not rise above the level of mediocrity; patience and perseverance were his strong points, but the most powerful sentiment in him was ambition, the desire to get into good society, not to be inferior to others in spite of fortune. He had studied diligently and gone to the Dorpat University from ambition. Poverty exasperated him, and made him watchful and cunning. He expressed himself with originality; from his youth he had adopted a special kind of stinging and exasperated eloquence. His ideas did not rise above the common level; but his way of speaking made him seem not only a clever, but even a very clever, man. Having taken his degree as candidate, Pigasov decided to devote himself to the scholastic profession; he understood that in any other career he could not possibly be the equal of his associates. He tried to select them from a higher rank and knew how to gain their good graces; even by flattery, though he was always abusing them. But to do this he had not, to speak plainly, enough raw material. Having educated himself through no love for study, Pigasov knew very little thoroughly. He broke down miserably in the public disputation, while another student who had shared the same room with him, and who was constantly the subject of his ridicule, a man of very limited ability who had received a careful and solid education, gained a complete triumph. Pigasov was infuriated by this failure, he threw all his books and manuscripts into the fire and went into a government office. At first he did not get on badly, he made a fair official, not very active, extremely self-confident and bold, however; but he wanted to make his way more quickly, he made a false step, got into trouble, and was obliged to retire from the service. He spent three years on the property he had bought himself and suddenly married a wealthy half-educated woman who was captivated by his unceremonious and sarcastic manners. But Pigasov's character had become so soured and irritable that family life was unendurable to him. After living with him a few years, his wife went off secretly to Moscow and sold her estate to an enterprising speculator; Pigasov had only just finished building a house on it. Utterly crushed by this last blow, Pigasov began a lawsuit with his wife, but gained nothing by it. After this he lived in solitude, and went to see his neighbours, whom he abused behind their backs and even to their faces, and who welcomed him with a kind of constrained half-laugh, though he did not inspire them with any serious dread. He never took a book in his hand. He had about a hundred serfs; his peasants were not badly off.

'Ah! *Constantin*,' said Darya Mihailovna, when Pandalevsky came into the drawing-room, 'is *Alexandrine* coming?'

'Alexandra Pavlovna asked me to thank you, and they will be extremely delighted,' replied Konstantin Diomiditch, bowing affably in all directions, and running his plump white hand with its triangular cut nails through his faultlessly arranged hair.

'And is Volintsev coming too?'

'Yes.'

'So, according to you, African Semenitch,' continued Darya Mihailovna, turning to Pigasov, 'all young ladies are affected?'

Pigasov's mouth twitched, and he plucked nervously at his elbow.

'I say,' he began in a measured voice—in his most violent moods of exasperation he always spoke slowly and precisely. 'I say that young ladies, in general—of present company, of course, I say nothing.'

'But that does not prevent your thinking of them,' put in Darya Mihailovna.

'I say nothing of them,' repeated Pigasov. 'All young ladies, in general, are affected to the most extreme point—affected in the expression of their feelings. If a young lady is frightened, for instance, or pleased with anything, or distressed, she is certain first to throw her person into some such elegant attitude (and Pigasov threw his figure into an unbecoming pose and spread out his hands) and then she shrieks—ah! or she laughs or cries. I did once though (and here Pigasov smiled complacently) succeed in eliciting a genuine, unaffected expression of emotion from a remarkably affected young lady!'

'How did you do that?'

Pigasov's eyes sparkled.

'I poked her in the side with an aspen stake, from behind. She did shriek, and I said to her, "Bravo, bravo! that's the voice of nature, that was a genuine shriek! Always do like that for the future!"'

Every one in the room laughed.

'What nonsense you talk, African Semenitch,' cried Darya Mihailovna. 'Am I to believe that you would poke a girl in the side with a stake!'

'Yes, indeed, with a stake, a very big stake, like those that are used in the defence of a fort.'

'*Mais c'est un horreur ce que vous dites là, Monsieur,*' cried Mlle. Boncourt, looking angrily at the boys, who were in fits of laughter.

'Oh, you mustn't believe him,' said Darya Mihailovna. 'Don't you know him?'

But the offended French lady could not be pacified for a long while, and kept muttering something to herself.

'You need not believe me,' continued Pigasov coolly, 'but I assure you I told the simple truth. Who should know if not I? After that perhaps you won't believe that our neighbour, Madame Tchepuz, Elena Antonovna, told me herself, mind *herself*, that she had murdered her nephew?'

'What an invention!'

'Wait a minute, wait a minute! Listen and judge for yourselves. Mind, I don't want to slander her, I even like her as far as one can like a woman. She hasn't a single book in her house except a calendar, and she can't read except aloud, and that exercise throws her into a violent perspiration, and she complains then that her eyes feel bursting out of her head.... In short, she's a capital woman, and her servant girls grow fat. Why should I slander her?'

'You see,' observed Darya Mihailovna, 'African Semenitch has got on his hobbyhorse, now he will not be off it to-night.'

'My hobby! But women have three at least, which they are never off, except, perhaps, when they're asleep.'

'What three hobbies are those?'

'Reproof, reproach, recrimination.'

'Do you know, African Semenitch,' began Darya Mihailovna, 'you cannot be so bitter against women for nothing. Some woman or other must have——'

'Done me an injury, you mean?' Pigasov interrupted.

Darya Mihailovna was rather embarrassed; she remembered Pigasov's unlucky marriage, and only nodded.

'One woman certainly did me an injury,' said Pigasov, 'though she was a good, very good one.'

'Who was that?'

'My mother,' said Pigasov, dropping his voice.

'Your mother? What injury could she have done you?'

'She brought me into the world.'

Darya Mihailovna frowned.

'Our conversation,' she said, 'seems to have taken a gloomy turn. *Constantin*, play us Thalberg's new *étude*. I daresay the music will soothe African Semenitch. Orpheus soothed savage beasts.'

Konstantin Diomiditch took his seat at the piano, and played the étude very fairly well. Natalya Alexyevna at first listened attentively, then she bent over her work again.

'*Merci, c'est charmant*,' observed Darya Mihailovna, 'I love Thalberg. *Il est si distingué*. What are you thinking of, African Semenitch?'

'I thought,' began African Semenitch slowly, 'that there are three kinds of egoists; the egoists who live themselves and let others live; the egoists who live themselves and don't let others live; and the egoists who don't live themselves and don't let others live. Women, for the most part, belong to the third class.'

'That's polite! I am very much astonished at one thing, African Semenitch; your confidence in your convictions; of course you can never be mistaken.'

'Who says so? I make mistakes; a man, too, may be mistaken. But do you know the difference between a man's mistakes and a woman's? Don't you know? Well, here it is; a man may say, for example, that twice two makes not four, but five, or three and a half; but a woman will say that twice two makes a wax candle.'

'I fancy I've heard you say that before. But allow me to ask what connection had your idea of the three kinds of egoists with the music you have just been hearing?'

'None at all, but I did not listen to the music.'

'Well, "incurable I see you are, and that is all about it,"' answered Darya Mihailovna, slightly altering Griboyedov's line. 'What do you like, since you don't care for music? Literature?'

'I like literature, only not our contemporary literature.'

'Why?'

'I'll tell you why. I crossed the Oka lately in a ferry boat with a gentleman. The ferry got fixed in a narrow place; they had to drag the carriages ashore by hand. This gentleman had a very heavy coach. While the ferrymen were straining themselves to drag the coach on to the bank, the gentleman groaned so, standing in the ferry, that one felt quite sorry for him.... Well, I thought, here's a fresh illustration of the system of division of labour! That's just like our modern literature; other people do the work, and it does the groaning.'

Darya Mihailovna smiled.

'And that is called expressing contemporary life,' continued Pigasov indefatigably, 'profound sympathy with the social question and so on. ... Oh, how I hate those grand words!'

'Well, the women you attack so—they at least don't use grand words.'

Pigasov shrugged his shoulders.

'They don't use them because they don't understand them.'

Darya Mihailovna flushed slightly.

'You are beginning to be impertinent, African Semenitch!' she remarked with a forced smile.

There was complete stillness in the room.

'Where is Zolotonosha?' asked one of the boys suddenly of Bassistoff.

'In the province of Poltava, my dear boy,' replied Pigasov, 'in the centre of Little Russia.' (He was glad of an opportunity of changing the conversation.) 'We were talking of literature,' he continued, 'if I had money to spare, I would at once become a Little Russian poet.'

'What next? a fine poet you would make!' retorted Darya Mihailovna. 'Do you know Little Russian?'

'Not a bit; but it isn't necessary.'

'Not necessary?'

'Oh no, it's not necessary. You need only take a sheet of paper and write at the top "A Ballad," then begin like this, "Heigho, alack, my destiny!" or "the Cossack Nalivaiko was sitting on a hill and then on the mountain, under the green tree the birds are singing, grae, voropae, gop, gop!" or something of that kind. And the thing's done. Print it and publish it. The Little Russian will read it, drop his head into his hands and infallibly burst into tears—he is such a sensitive soul!'

'Good heavens!' cried Bassistoff. 'What are you saying? It's too absurd for anything. I have lived in Little Russia, I love it and know the language... "grae, grae, voropae" is absolute nonsense.'

'It may be, but the Little Russian will weep all the same. You speak of the "language."... But is there a Little Russian language? Is it a language, in your opinion? an independent language? I would pound my best friend in a mortar before I'd agree to that.'

Bassistoff was about to retort.

'Leave him alone!' said Darya Mihailovna, 'you know that you will hear nothing but paradoxes from him.'

Pigasov smiled ironically. A footman came in and announced the arrival of Alexandra Pavlovna and her brother.

Darya Mihailovna rose to meet her guests.

'How do you do, Alexandrine?' she began, going up to her, 'how good of you to come!... How are you, Sergei Pavlitch?'

Volintsev shook hands with Darya Mihailovna and went up to Natalya Alexyevna.

'But how about that baron, your new acquaintance, is he coming to-day?' asked Pigasov.

'Yes, he is coming.'

'He is a great philosopher, they say; he is just brimming over with Hegel, I suppose?'

Darya Mihailovna made no reply, and making Alexandra Pavlovna sit down on the sofa, established herself near her.

'Philosophies,' continued Pigasov, 'are elevated points of view! That's another abomination of mine; these elevated points of view. And what can one see from above? Upon my soul, if you want to buy a horse, you don't look at it from a steeple!'

'This baron was going to bring you an essay?' said Alexandra Pavlovna.

'Yes, an essay,' replied Darya Mihailovna, with exaggerated carelessness, 'on the relation of commerce to manufactures in Russia. ... But don't be afraid; we will not read it here.... I did not invite you for that. *Le baron est aussi aimable que savant.* And he speaks Russian beautifully! *C'est un vrai torrent... il vous entraîne.*

'He speaks Russian so beautifully,' grumbled Pigasov, 'that he deserves a eulogy in French.'

'You may grumble as you please, African Semenitch.... It's in keeping with your ruffled locks.... I wonder, though, why he does not come. Do you know what, *messieurs et mesdames*' added Darya Mihailovna, looking round, 'we will go into the garden. There is still nearly an hour to dinner-time and the weather is glorious.'

All the company rose and went into the garden.

Darya Mihailovna's garden stretched right down to the river. There were many alleys of old lime-trees in it, full of sunlight and shade and fragrance and glimpses of emerald green at the ends of the walks, and many arbours of acacias and lilacs.

Volintsev turned into the thickest part of the garden with Natalya and Mlle. Boncourt. He walked beside Natalya in silence. Mlle. Boncourt followed a little behind.

'What have you been doing to-day?' asked Volintsev at last, pulling the ends of his handsome dark brown moustache.

In features he resembled his sister strikingly; but there was less movement and life in his expression, and his soft beautiful eyes had a melancholy look.

'Oh! nothing,' answered Natalya, 'I have been listening to Pigasov's sarcasms, I have done some embroidery on canvas, and I've been reading.'

'And what have you been reading?'

'Oh! I read—a history of the Crusades,' said Natalya, with some hesitation.

Volintsev looked at her.

'Ah!' he ejaculated at last, 'that must be interesting.'

He picked a twig and began to twirl it in the air. They walked another twenty paces.

'What is this baron whom your mother has made acquaintance with?' began Volintsev again.

'A Gentleman of the Bedchamber, a new arrival; *maman* speaks very highly of him.'

'Your mother is quick to take fancies to people.'

'That shows that her heart is still young,' observed Natalya.

'Yes. I shall soon bring you your mare. She is almost quite broken in now. I want to teach her to gallop, and I shall manage it soon.'

'*Merci*!... But I'm quite ashamed. You are breaking her in yourself ... and they say it's so hard!'

'To give you the least pleasure, you know, Natalya Alexyevna, I am ready... I... not in such trifles——'

Volintsev grew confused.

Natalya looked at him with friendly encouragement, and again said '*merci*!'

'You know,' continued Sergei Pavlitch after a long pause, 'that not such things.... But why am I saying this? you know everything, of course.'

At that instant a bell rang in the house.

'Ah! *la cloche du diner*!' cried Mlle. Boncourt, '*rentrons*.'

'*Quel dommage*,' thought the old French lady to herself as she mounted the balcony steps behind Volintsev and Natalya, '*quel dommage que ce charmant garçon ait si peu de ressources dans la conversation*,' which may be translated, 'you are a good fellow, my dear boy, but rather a fool.'

The baron did not arrive to dinner. They waited half-an-hour for him. Conversation flagged at the table. Sergei Pavlitch did nothing but gaze at Natalya, near whom he was sitting, and zealously filled up her glass with water. Pandalevsky tried in vain to entertain his neighbour, Alexandra Pavlovna; he was bubbling over with sweetness, but she hardly refrained from yawning.

Bassistoff was rolling up pellets of bread and thinking of nothing at all; even Pigasov was silent, and when Darya Mihailovna remarked to him that he had not been very polite to-day, he replied crossly, 'When am I polite? that's not in my line;' and smiling grimly he added, 'have a little patience; I am only kvas, you know, *du simple* Russian kvas; but your Gentleman of the Bedchamber——'

'Bravo!' cried Darya Mihailovna, 'Pigasov is jealous, he is jealous already!'

But Pigasov made her no rejoinder, and only gave her a rather cross look.

Seven o'clock struck, and they were all assembled again in the drawing-room.

'He is not coming, clearly,' said Darya Mihailovna.

But, behold, the rumble of a carriage was heard: a small tarantass drove into the court, and a few instants later a footman entered the drawing-room and gave Darya Mihailovna a note on a silver salver. She glanced through it, and turning to the footman asked:

'But where is the gentleman who brought this letter?'

'He is sitting in the carriage. Shall I ask him to come up?'

'Ask him to do so.'

The man went out.

'Fancy, how vexatious!' continued Darya Mihailovna, 'the baron has received a summons to return at once to Petersburg. He has sent me his essay by a certain Mr. Rudin, a friend of his. The baron wanted to introduce him to me—he speaks very highly of him. But how vexatious it is! I had hoped the baron would stay here for some time.'

'Dmitri Nikolaitch Rudin,' announced the servant

III

A man of about thirty-five entered, of a tall, somewhat stooping figure, with crisp curly hair and swarthy complexion, an irregular but expressive and intelligent face, a liquid brilliance in his quick, dark blue eyes, a straight, broad nose, and well-curved lips. His clothes were not new, and were somewhat small, as though he had outgrown them.

He walked quickly up to Darya Mihailovna, and with a slight bow told her that he had long wished to have the honour of an introduction to her, and that his friend the baron greatly regretted that he could not take leave of her in person.

The thin sound of Rudin's voice seemed out of keeping with his tall figure and broad chest.

'Pray be seated... very delighted,' murmured Darya Mihailovna, and, after introducing him to the rest of the company, she asked him whether he belonged to those parts or was a visitor.

'My estate is in the T—— province,' replied Rudin, holding his hat on his knees. 'I have not been here long. I came on business and stayed for a while in your district town.'

'With whom?'

'With the doctor. He was an old chum of mine at the university.'

'Ah! the doctor. He is highly spoken of. He is skilful in his work, they say. But have you known the baron long?'

'I met him last winter in Moscow, and I have just been spending about a week with him.'

'He is a very clever man, the baron.'

'Yes.'

Darya Mihailovna sniffed at her little crushed-up handkerchief steeped in *eau de cologne*.

'Are you in the government service?' she asked.

'Who? I?'

'Yes.'

'No. I have retired.'

There followed a brief pause. The general conversation was resumed.

'If you will allow me to be inquisitive,' began Pigasov, turning to Rudin, 'do you know the contents of the essay which his excellency the baron has sent?'

'Yes, I do.'

'This essay deals with the relations to commerce—or no, of manufactures to commerce in our country.... That was your expression, I think, Darya Mihailovna?'

'Yes, it deals with'... began Darya Mihailovna, pressing her hand to her forehead.

'I am, of course, a poor judge of such matters,' continued Pigasov, 'but I must confess that to me even the title of the essay seems excessively (how could I put it delicately?) excessively obscure and complicated.'

'Why does it seem so to you?'

Pigasov smiled and looked across at Darya Mihailovna.

'Why, is it clear to you?' he said, turning his foxy face again towards Rudin.

'To me? Yes.'

'H'm. No doubt you must know better.'

'Does your head ache?' Alexandra Pavlovna inquired of Darya Mihailovna.

'No. It is only my—*c'est nerveux.*'

'Allow me to inquire,' Pigasov was beginning again in his nasal tones, 'your friend, his excellency Baron Muffel—I think that's his name?'

'Precisely.'

'Does his excellency Baron Muffel make a special study of political economy, or does he only devote to that interesting subject the hours of leisure left over from his social amusements and his official duties?'

Rudin looked steadily at Pigasov.

'The baron is an amateur on this subject,' he replied, growing rather red, 'but in his essay there is much that is interesting and just.'

'I am not able to dispute it with you; I have not read the essay. But I venture to ask—the work of your friend Baron Muffel is no doubt founded more upon general propositions than upon facts?'

'It contains both facts and propositions founded upon the facts.'

'Yes, yes. I must tell you that, in my opinion—and I've a right to give my opinion, on occasion; I spent three years at Dorpat... all these, so-called general propositions, hypotheses, these systems—excuse me, I am a provincial, I speak the truth bluntly—are absolutely worthless. All that's only theorising—only good for misleading people. Give us facts, sir, and that's enough!'

'Really!' retorted Rudin, 'why, but ought not one to give the significance of the facts?'

'General propositions,' continued Pigasov, 'they're my abomination, these general propositions, theories, conclusions. All that's based on so-called convictions; every one is talking about his convictions, and attaches importance to them, prides himself on them. Ah!'

And Pigasov shook his fist in the air. Pandalevsky laughed.

'Capital!' put in Rudin, 'it follows that there is no such thing as conviction according to you?'

'No, it doesn't exist.'

'Is that your conviction?'

'Yes.'

'How do you say that there are none then? Here you have one at the very first turn.'

All in the room smiled and looked at one another.

'One minute, one minute, but——,' Pigasov was beginning.

But Darya Mihailovna clapped her hands crying, 'Bravo, bravo, Pigasov's beaten!' and she gently took Rudin's hat from his hand.

'Defer your delight a little, madam; there's plenty of time!' Pigasov began with annoyance. 'It's not sufficient to say a witty word, with a show of superiority; you must prove, refute. We had wandered from the subject of our discussion.'

'With your permission,' remarked Rudin, coolly, 'the matter is very simple. You do not believe in the value of general propositions—you do not believe in convictions?'

'I don't believe in them, I don't believe in anything!'

'Very good. You are a sceptic.'

'I see no necessity for using such a learned word. However——'

'Don't interrupt!' interposed Darya Mihailovna.

'At him, good dog!' Pandalevsky said to himself at the same instant, and smiled all over.

'That word expresses my meaning,' pursued Rudin. 'You understand it; why not make use of it? You don't believe in anything. Why do you believe in facts?'

'Why? That's good! Facts are matters of experience, every one knows what facts are. I judge of them by experience, by my own senses.'

'But may not your senses deceive you? Your senses tell you that the sun goes round the earth,... but perhaps you don't agree with Copernicus? You don't even believe in him?'

Again a smile passed over every one's face, and all eyes were fastened on Rudin. 'He's by no means a fool,' every one was thinking.

'You are pleased to keep on joking,' said Pigasov. 'Of course that's very original, but it's not to the point.'

'In what I have said hitherto,' rejoined Rudin, 'there is, unfortunately, too little that's original. All that has been well known a very long time, and has been said a thousand times. That is not the pith of the matter.'

'What is then?' asked Pigasov, not without insolence.

In discussions he always first bantered his opponent, then grew cross, and finally sulked and was silent.

'Here it is,' continued Rudin. 'I cannot help, I own, feeling sincere regret when I hear sensible people attack——'

'Systems?' interposed Pigasov.

'Yes, with your leave, even systems. What frightens you so much in that word? Every system is founded on a knowledge of fundamental laws, the principles of life——'

'But there is no knowing them, no discovering them.'

'One minute. Doubtless they are not easy for every one to get at, and to make mistakes is natural to man. However, you will certainly agree with me that Newton, for example, discovered some at least of these fundamental laws? He was a genius, we grant you; but the grandeur of the discoveries of genius is that they become the heritage of all. The effort to discover universal principles in the multiplicity of phenomena is one of the radical characteristics of human thought, and all our civilisation——'

'That's what you're driving at!' Pigasov broke in in a drawling tone. 'I am a practical man and all these metaphysical subtleties I don't enter into and don't want to enter into.'

'Very good! That's as you prefer. But take note that your very desire to be exclusively a practical man is itself your sort of system—your theory.'

'Civilisation you talk about!' blurted in Pigasov; 'that's another admirable notion of yours! Much use in it, this vaunted civilisation! I would not give a brass farthing for your civilisation!'

'But what a poor sort of argument, African Semenitch!' observed Darya Mihailovna, inwardly much pleased by the calmness and perfect good-breeding of her new acquaintance. '*C'est un homme comme il faut*,' she thought, looking with well-disposed scrutiny at Rudin; 'we must be nice to him!' Those last words she mentally pronounced in Russian.

'I will not champion civilisation,' continued Rudin after a short pause, 'it does not need my championship. You don't like it, every one to his own taste. Besides, that would take us too far. Allow me only to remind you of the old saying, "Jupiter, you are angry; therefore you are in the wrong." I meant to say that all those onslaughts upon systems—general propositions—are especially distressing, because together with these systems men repudiate knowledge in general, and all science and faith in it, and consequently also faith in themselves, in their own powers. But this faith is essential to men; they cannot exist by their sensations alone, they are wrong to fear ideas and not to trust in them. Scepticism is always characterised by barrenness and impotence.'

'That's all words!' muttered Pigasov.

'Perhaps so. But allow me to point out to you that when we say "that's all words!" we often wish ourselves to avoid the necessity of saying anything more substantial than mere words.'

'What?' said Pigasov, winking his eyes.

'You understood what I meant,' retorted Rudin, with involuntary, but instantly repressed impatience. 'I repeat, if man has no steady principle in which he trusts, no ground on which he can take a firm stand, how can he form a just estimate of the needs, the tendencies and the future of his country? How can he know what he ought to do, if——'

'I leave you the field,' ejaculated Pigasov abruptly, and with a bow he turned away without looking at any one.

Rudin stared at him, and smiled slightly, saying nothing.

'Aha! he has taken to flight!' said Darya Mihailovna. 'Never mind, Dmitri...! I beg your pardon,' she added with a cordial smile, 'what is your paternal name?'

'Nikolaitch.'

'Never mind, my dear Dmitri Nikolaitch, he did not deceive any of us. He wants to make a show of not *wishing* to argue any more. He is conscious that he *cannot* argue with you. But you had better sit nearer to us and let us have a little talk.'

Rudin moved his chair up.

'How is it we have not met till now?' was Darya Mihailovna's question. 'That is what surprises me. Have you read this book? *C'est de Tocqueville, vous savez?*'

And Darya Mihailovna held out the French pamphlet to Rudin.

Rudin took the thin volume in his hand, turned over a few pages of it, and laying it down on the table, replied that he had not read that particular work of M. de Tocqueville, but that he had often reflected on the question treated by him. A conversation began to spring up. Rudin seemed uncertain at first, and not disposed to speak out freely; his words did not come readily, but at last he grew warm and began to speak. In a quarter of an hour his voice was the only sound in the room, All were crowding in a circle round him.

Only Pigasov remained aloof, in a corner by the fireplace. Rudin spoke with intelligence, with fire and with judgment; he showed much learning, wide reading. No one had expected to find in him a remarkable man. His clothes were so shabby, so little was known of him. Every one felt it strange and incomprehensible that such a clever man should have suddenly made his appearance in the country. He seemed all the more wonderful and, one may even say, fascinating to all of them, beginning with Darya Mihailovna. She was pluming herself on having discovered him, and already at this early date was dreaming of how she would introduce Rudin into the world. In her quickness to receive impressions there was much that was almost childish, in spite of her years. Alexandra Pavlovna, to tell the truth, understood little of all that Rudin said, but was full of wonder and delight; her brother too was admiring him. Pandalevsky was watching Darya Mihailovna and was filled with envy. Pigasov thought, 'If I have to give five hundred roubles I will get a nightingale to sing better than that!' But the most impressed of all the party were Bassistoff and Natalya. Scarcely a breath escaped Bassistoff; he sat the whole time with open mouth and round eyes and listened—listened as he had never listened to any one in his life—while Natalya's face was suffused by a crimson flush, and her eyes, fastened unwaveringly on Rudin, were both dimmed and shining.

'What splendid eyes he has!' Volintsev whispered to her.

'Yes, they are.'

'It's only a pity his hands are so big and red.'

Natalya made no reply.

Tea was brought in. The conversation became more general, but still by the sudden unanimity with which every one was silent, directly Rudin opened his mouth, one could judge of the strength of the impression he had produced. Darya Mihailovna suddenly felt inclined to tease Pigasov. She went up to him and said in an undertone, 'Why don't you speak instead of doing nothing but smile sarcastically? Make an effort, challenge him again,' and without waiting for him to answer, she beckoned to Rudin.

'There's one thing more you don't know about him,' she said to him, with a gesture towards Pigasov,—'he is a terrible hater of women, he is always attacking them; pray, show him the true path.'

Rudin involuntarily looked down upon Pigasov; he was a head and shoulders taller. Pigasov almost withered up with fury, and his sour face grew pale.

'Darya Mihailovna is mistaken,' he said in an unsteady voice, 'I do not only attack women; I am not a great admirer of the whole human species.'

'What can have given you such a poor opinion of them?' inquired Rudin.

Pigasov looked him straight in the face.

'The study of my own heart, no doubt, in which I find every day more and more that is base. I judge of others by myself. Possibly this too is erroneous, and I am far worse than others, but what am I to do? it's a habit!'

'I understand you and sympathise with you!' was Rudin's rejoinder. 'What generous soul has not experienced a yearning for self-humiliation? But one ought not to remain in that condition from which there is no outlet beyond.'

'I am deeply indebted for the certificate of generosity you confer on my soul,' retorted Pigasov. 'As for my condition, there's not much amiss with it, so that even if there were an outlet from it, it might go to the deuce, I shouldn't look for it!'

'But that means—pardon the expression—to prefer the gratification of your own pride to the desire to be and live in the truth.'

'Undoubtedly,' cried Pigasov, 'pride—that I understand, and you, I expect, understand, and every one understands; but truth, what is truth? Where is it, this truth?'

'You are repeating yourself, let me warn you,' remarked Darya Mihailovna.

Pigasov shrugged his shoulders.

'Well, where's the harm if I do? I ask: where is truth? Even the philosophers don't know what it is. Kant says it is one thing; but Hegel—no, you're wrong, it's something else.'

'And do you know what Hegel says of it?' asked Rudin, without raising his voice.

'I repeat,' continued Pigasov, flying into a passion, 'that I cannot understand what truth means. According to my idea, it doesn't exist at all in the world, that is to say, the word exists but not the thing itself.'

'Fie, fie!' cried Darya Mihailovna, 'I wonder you're not ashamed to say so, you old sinner! No truth? What is there to live for in the world after that?'

'Well, I go so far as to think, Darya Mihailovna,' retorted Pigasov, in a tone of annoyance, 'that it would be much easier for you, in any case, to live without truth than without your cook, Stepan, who is such a master hand at soups! And what do you want with truth, kindly tell me? you can't trim a bonnet with it!'

'A joke is not an argument,' observed Darya Mihailovna, 'especially when you descend to personal insult.'

'I don't know about truth, but I see speaking it does not answer,' muttered Pigasov, and he turned angrily away.

And Rudin began to speak of pride, and he spoke well. He showed that man without pride is worthless, that pride is the lever by which the earth can be moved from its foundations, but that at the same time he alone deserves the name of man who knows how to control his pride, as the rider does his horse, who offers up his own personality as a sacrifice to the general good.

'Egoism,' so he ended, 'is suicide. The egoist withers like a solitary barren tree; but pride, ambition, as the active effort after perfection, is the source of all that is great.... Yes! a man must prune away the stubborn egoism of his personality to give it the right of self-expression.'

'Can you lend me a pencil?' Pigasov asked Bassistoff.

Bassistoff did not at once understand what Pigasov had asked him.

'What do you want a pencil for?' he said at last

'I want to write down Mr. Rudin's last sentence. If one doesn't write it down, one might forget it, I'm afraid! But you will own, a sentence like that is such a handful of trumps.'

'There are things which it is a shame to laugh at and make fun of, African Semenitch!' said Bassistoff warmly, turning away from Pigasov.

Meanwhile Rudin had approached Natalya. She got up; her face expressed her confusion. Volintsev, who was sitting near her, got up too.

'I see a piano,' began Rudin, with the gentle courtesy of a travelling prince; 'don't you play on it?'

'Yes, I play,' replied Natalya, 'but not very well. Here is Konstantin Diomiditch plays much better than I do.'

Pandalevsky put himself forward with a simper. 'You should not say that, Natalya Alexyevna; your playing is not at all inferior to mine.'

'Do you know Schubert's "Erlkonig"?' asked Rudin.

'He knows it, he knows it!' interposed Darya Mihailovna. 'Sit down, Konstantin. You are fond of music, Dmitri Nikolaitch?'

Rudin only made a slight motion of the head and ran his hand through his hair, as though disposing himself to listen. Pandalevsky began to play.

Natalya was standing near the piano, directly facing Rudin. At the first sound his face was transfigured. His dark blue eyes moved slowly about, from time to time resting upon Natalya. Pandalevsky finished playing.

Rudin said nothing and walked up to the open window. A fragrant mist lay like a soft shroud over the garden; a drowsy scent breathed from the trees near. The stars shed a mild radiance. The summer night was soft—and softened all. Rudin gazed into the dark garden, and looked round.

'That music and this night,' he began, 'reminded me of my student days in Germany; our meetings, our serenades.'

'You have been in Germany then?' said Darya Mihailovna.

'I spent a year at Heidelberg, and nearly a year at Berlin.'

'And did you dress as a student? They say they wear a special dress there.'

'At Heidelberg I wore high boots with spurs, and a hussar's jacket with braid on it, and I let my hair grow to my shoulders. In Berlin the students dress like everybody else.'

'Tell us something of your student life,' said Alexandra Pavlovna.

Rudin complied. He was not altogether successful in narrative. There was a lack of colour in his descriptions. He did not know how to be humorous. However, from relating his own adventures abroad, Rudin soon passed to general themes, the special value of education and science, universities, and university life generally. He sketched in a large and comprehensive picture in broad and striking lines. All listened to him with profound attention. His eloquence was masterly and attractive, not altogether clear, but even this want of clearness added a special charm to his words.

The exuberance of his thought hindered Rudin from expressing himself definitely and exactly. Images followed upon images; comparisons started up one after another—now startlingly bold, now strikingly true. It was not the complacent effort of the practised speaker, but the very breath of inspiration that was felt in his impatient improvising. He did not seek out his words; they came obediently and spontaneously to his lips, and each word seemed to flow straight from his soul, and was burning with all the fire of conviction. Rudin was the master of almost the greatest secret—the music of eloquence. He knew how in striking one chord of the heart to set all the others vaguely quivering and resounding. Many of his listeners, perhaps, did not understand very precisely what his eloquence was about; but their bosoms heaved, it seemed as though veils were lifted before their eyes, something radiant, glorious, seemed shimmering in the distance.

All Rudin's thoughts seemed centred on the future; this lent him something of the impetuous dash of youth... Standing at the window, not looking at any one in special, he spoke, and inspired by the general sympathy and attention, the presence of young women, the beauty of the night, carried along by the tide of his own emotions, he rose to the height of eloquence, of poetry.... The very sound of his voice, intense and soft, increased the fascination; it seemed as though some higher power were speaking through his lips, startling even to himself.... Rudin spoke of what lends eternal significance to the fleeting life of man.

'I remember a Scandinavian legend,' thus he concluded, 'a king is sitting with his warriors round the fire in a long dark barn. It was night and winter. Suddenly a little bird flew in at the open door and flew out again at the other. The king spoke and said that this bird is like man in the world; it flew in from darkness and out again into darkness, and was not long in the warmth and light.... "King," replies the oldest of the warriors, "even in the dark the bird is not lost, but finds her nest." Even so our life is short and worthless; but all that is great is accomplished through men. The consciousness of being the instrument of these higher powers ought to outweigh all other joys for man; even in death he finds his life, his nest.'

Rudin stopped and dropped his eyes with a smile of involuntary embarrassment.

'*Vous êtes un poète*,' was Darya Mihailovna's comment in an undertone. And all were inwardly agreeing with her—all except Pigasov. Without waiting for the end of Rudin's long speech, he quietly took his hat and as he went out whispered viciously to Pandalevsky who was standing near the door:

'No! Fools are more to my taste.'

No one, however, tried to detain him or even noticed his absence.

The servants brought in supper, and half an hour later, all had taken leave and separated. Darya Mihailovna begged Rudin to remain the night. Alexandra Pavlovna, as she went home in the carriage with her brother, several times fell to exclaiming and marvelling at the extraordinary cleverness of Rudin. Volintsev agreed with her, though he observed that he sometimes expressed himself somewhat obscurely—that is to say, not altogether intelligibly, he added,—wishing, no doubt, to make his own thought clear, but his face was gloomy, and his eyes, fixed on a corner of the carriage, seemed even more melancholy than usual.

Pandalevsky went to bed, and as he took off his daintily embroidered braces, he said aloud 'A very smart fellow!' and suddenly, looking harshly at his page, ordered him out of the room. Bassistoff did not sleep the whole night and did not undress—he was writing till morning a letter to a comrade of his in Moscow; and Natalya, too, though she undressed and lay down in her bed, had not an instant's sleep and never closed her eyes. With her head propped on her arm, she gazed fixedly into the darkness; her veins were throbbing feverishly and her bosom often heaved with a deep sigh.

IV

The next morning Rudin had only just finished dressing when a servant came to him with an invitation from Darya Mihailovna to come to her boudoir and drink tea with her. Rudin found her alone. She greeted him very cordially, inquired whether he had passed a good night, poured him out a cup of tea with her own hands, asked him whether there was sugar enough in it, offered him a cigarette, and twice again repeated that she was surprised that she had not met him long before. Rudin was about to take a seat some distance away; but Darya Mihailovna motioned him to an easy chair, which stood near her lounge, and bending a little towards him began to question him about his family, his plans and intentions. Darya Mihailovna spoke carelessly and listened with an air of indifference; but it was perfectly evident to Rudin that she was laying herself out to please him, even to flatter him. It was not for nothing that she had arranged this morning interview, and had dressed so simply yet elegantly *a la Madame Récamier!* But Darya Mihailovna soon left off questioning him. She began to tell him about herself, her youth, and the people she had known. Rudin gave a sympathetic attention to her lucubrations, though—a curious fact—whatever personage Darya Mihailovna might be talking about, she always stood in the foreground, she alone, and the personage seemed to be effaced, to slink away in the background, and to disappear. But to make up for that, Rudin learnt in full detail precisely what Darya Mihailovna had said to a certain distinguished statesman, and what influence she had had on such and such a celebrated poet. To judge from Darya Mihailovna's accounts, one might fancy that all the distinguished men of the last five-and-twenty years had dreamt of nothing but how they could make her acquaintance, and gain her good opinion. She spoke of them simply, without particular enthusiasm or admiration, as though they were her daily associates, calling some of them queer fellows. As she talked of them, like a rich setting round a worthless stone, their names ranged themselves in a brilliant circlet round the principal name—around Darya Mihailovna.

Rudin listened, smoking a cigarette, and said little. He could speak well and liked speaking; carrying on a conversation was not in his line, though he was also a good listener. All men—if only they had not been intimidated by him to begin with—opened their hearts with confidence in his presence; he followed the thread of another man's narrative so readily and sympathetically. He had a great deal of good-nature—that special good-nature of which men are full, who are accustomed to feel themselves superior to others. In arguments he seldom allowed his antagonist to express himself fully, he crushed him by his eager, vehement and passionate dialectic.

Darya Mihailovna expressed herself in Russian. She prided herself on her knowledge of her own language, though French words and expressions often escaped her. She intentionally made use of simple popular terms of speech; but not always successfully. Rudin's ear was not outraged by the strange medley of language on Darya Mihailovna's lips, indeed he hardly had an ear for it.

Darya Mihailovna was exhausted at last and letting her head fall on the cushions of her easy-chair she fixed her eyes on Rudin and was silent.

'I understand now,' began Rudin, speaking slowly, 'I understand why you come every summer into the country. This period of rest is essential for you; the peace of the country after your life in the capital refreshes and strengthens you. I am convinced that you must be profoundly sensitive to the beauties of nature.'

Darya Mihailovna gave Rudin a sidelong look.

'Nature—yes—yes—of course.... I am passionately fond of it; but do you know, Dmitri Nikolaitch, even in the country one cannot do without society. And here there is practically none. Pigasov is the most intelligent person here.'

'The cross old gentleman who was here last night?' inquired Rudin.

'Yes.... In the country though, even he is of use—he sometimes makes one laugh.'

'He is by no means stupid,' returned Rudin, 'but he is on the wrong path. I don't know whether you will agree with me, Darya Mihailovna, but in negation—in complete and universal negation—there is no salvation to be found? Deny everything and you will easily pass for a man of ability; it's a well-known trick. Simple-hearted people are quite ready to conclude that you are worth more than what you deny. And that's often an error. In the first place, you can pick holes in anything; and secondly, even if you are right in what you say, it's the worse for you; your intellect, directed by simple negation, grows colourless and withers up. While you gratify your vanity, you are deprived of the true consolations of thought; life—the essence of life— evades your petty and jaundiced criticism, and you end by scolding and becoming ridiculous. Only one who loves has the right to censure and find fault.'

'*Voilà, Monsieur Pigasov enteré*,' observed Darya Mihailovna. 'What a genius you have for defining a man! But Pigasov certainly would not have even understood you. He loves nothing but his own individuality.'

'And he finds fault with that so as to have the right to find fault with others,' Rudin put in.

Darya Mihailovna laughed.

"'He judges the sound,' as the saying is, "the sound by the sick." By the way, what do you think of the baron?'

'The baron? He is an excellent man, with a good heart and a knowledge ... but he has no character... and he will remain all his life half a savant, half a man of the world, that is to say, a dilettante, that is to say, to speak plainly,—neither one thing nor the other. ... But it's a pity!'

'That was my own idea,' observed Darya Mihailovna. 'I read his article.... *Entre nous... cela a assez peu de fond!*'

'Who else have you here?' asked Rudin, after a pause.

Darya Mihailovna knocked off the ash of her cigarette with her little finger.

'Oh, there is hardly any one else. Madame Lipin, Alexandra Pavlovna, whom you saw yesterday; she is very sweet—but that is all. Her brother is also a capital fellow—*un parfait honnête homme*. The Prince Garin you know. Those are all. There are two or three neighbours besides, but they are really good for nothing. They either give themselves airs or are unsociable, or else quite unsuitably free and easy. The ladies, as you know, I see nothing of. There is one other of our neighbours said to be a very cultivated, even a learned, man, but a dreadfully queer creature, a whimsical character. *Alexandrine* knows him, and I fancy is not indifferent to him.... Come, you ought to talk to her, Dmitri Nikolaitch; she's a sweet creature. She only wants developing.'

'I liked her very much,' remarked Rudin.

'A perfect child, Dmitri Nikolaitch, an absolute baby. She has been married, *mais c'est tout comme....* If I were a man, I should only fall in love with women like that.'

'Really?'

'Certainly. Such women are at least fresh, and freshness cannot be put on.'

'And can everything else?' Rudin asked, and he laughed—a thing which rarely happened with him. When he laughed his face assumed a strange, almost aged appearance, his eyes disappeared, his nose was wrinkled up.

'And who is this queer creature, as you call him, to whom Madame Lipin is not indifferent?' he asked.

'A certain Lezhnyov, Mihailo Mihailitch, a landowner here.'

Rudin seemed astonished; he raised his head.

'Lezhnyov—Mihailo Mihailitch?' he questioned. 'Is he a neighbour of yours?'

'Yes. Do you know him?'

Rudin did not speak for a minute.

'I used to know him long ago. He is a rich man, I suppose?' he added, pulling the fringe on his chair.

'Yes, he is rich, though he dresses shockingly, and drives in a racing droshky like a bailiff. I have been anxious to get him to come here; he is spoken of as clever; I have some business with him.... You know I manage my property myself.'

Rudin bowed assent.

'Yes; I manage it myself,' Darya Mihailovna continued. 'I don't introduce any foreign crazes, but prefer what is our own, what is Russian, and, as you see, things don't seem to do badly,' she added, with a wave of her hand.

'I have always been persuaded,' observed Rudin urbanely, 'of the absolutely mistaken position of those people who refuse to admit the practical intelligence of women.'

Darya Mihailovna smiled affably.

'You are very good to us,' was her comment 'But what was I going to say? What were we speaking of? Oh, yes; Lezhnyov: I have some business with him about a boundary. I have several times invited him here, and even to-day I am expecting him; but there's no knowing whether he'll come... he's such a strange creature.'

The curtain before the door was softly moved aside and the steward came in, a tall man, grey and bald, in a black coat, a white cravat, and a white waistcoat.

'What is it?' inquired Darya Mihailovna, and, turning a little towards Rudin, she added in a low voice, '*n'est ce pas, comme il ressemble à Canning?*'

'Mihailo Mihailitch Lezhnyov is here,' announced the steward. 'Will you see him?'

'Good Heavens!' exclaimed Darya Mihailovna, 'speak of the devil——ask him up.'

The steward went away.

'He's such an awkward creature. Now he has come, it's at the wrong moment; he has interrupted our talk.'

Rudin got up from his seat, but Darya Mihailovna stopped him.

'Where are you going? We can discuss the matter as well before you. And I want you to analyse him too, as you did Pigasov. When you talk, *vous gravez comme avec un burin.* Please stay.' Rudin was going to protest, but after a moment's thought he sat down.

Mihailo Mihailitch, whom the reader already knows, came into the room. He wore the same grey overcoat, and in his sunburnt hands he carried the same old foraging cap. He bowed tranquilly to Darya Mihailovna, and came up to the tea-table.

'At last you have favoured me with a visit, Monsieur Lezhnyov!' began Darya Mihailovna. 'Pray sit down. You are already acquainted, I hear,' she continued, with a gesture in Rudin's direction.

Lezhnyov looked at Rudin and smiled rather queerly.

'I know Mr. Rudin,' he assented, with a slight bow.

'We were together at the university,' observed Rudin in a low voice, dropping his eyes.

'And we met afterwards also,' remarked Lezhnyov coldly.

Darya Mihailovna looked at both in some perplexity and asked Lezhnyov to sit down. He sat down.

'You wanted to see me,' he began, 'on the subject of the boundary?'

'Yes; about the boundary. But I also wished to see you in any case. We are near neighbours, you know, and all but relations.'

'I am much obliged to you,' returned Lezhnyov. 'As regards the boundary, we have perfectly arranged that matter with your manager; I have agreed to all his proposals.'

'I knew that. But he told me that the contract could not be signed without a personal interview with you.'

'Yes; that is my rule. By the way, allow me to ask: all your peasants, I believe, pay rent?'

'Just so.'

'And you trouble yourself about boundaries! That's very praiseworthy.'

Lezhnyov did not speak for a minute.

'Well, I have come for a personal interview,' he said at last.

Darya Mihailovna smiled.

'I see you have come. You say that in such a tone.... You could not have been very anxious to come to see me.'

'I never go anywhere,' rejoined Lezhnyov phlegmatically.

'Not anywhere? But you go to see Alexandra Pavlovna.'

'I am an old friend of her brother's.'

'Her brother's! However, I never wish to force any one.... But pardon me, Mihailo Mihailitch, I am older than you, and I may be allowed to give you advice; what charm do you find in such an unsociable way of living? Or is my house in particular displeasing to you? You dislike me?'

'I don't know you, Darya Mihailovna, and so I can't dislike you. You have a splendid house; but I will confess to you frankly I don't like to have to stand on ceremony. And I haven't a respectable suit, I haven't any gloves, and I don't belong to your set.'

'By birth, by education, you belong to it, Mihailo Mihailitch! *vous êtes des notres.*'

'Birth and education are all very well, Darya Mihailovna; that's not the question.'

'A man ought to live with his fellows, Mihailo Mihailitch! What pleasure is there in sitting like Diogenes in his tub?'

'Well, to begin with, he was very well off there, and besides, how do you know I don't live with my fellows?'

Darya Mihailovna bit her lip.

'That's a different matter! It only remains for me to express my regret that I have not the honour of being included in the number of your friends.'

'Monsieur Lezhnyov,' put in Rudin, 'seems to carry to excess a laudable sentiment—the love of independence.'

Lezhnyov made no reply, he only looked at Rudin. A short silence followed.

'And so,' began Lezhnyov, getting up, 'I may consider our business as concluded, and tell your manager to send me the papers.'

'You may,... though I confess you are so uncivil I ought really to refuse you.'

'But you know this rearrangement of the boundary is far more in your interest than in mine.'

Darya Mihailovna shrugged her shoulders.

'You will not even have luncheon here?' she asked.

'Thank you; I never take luncheon, and I am in a hurry to get home.'

Darya Mihailovna got up.

'I will not detain you,' she said, going to the window. 'I will not venture to detain you.'

Lezhnyov began to take leave.

'Good-bye, Monsieur Lezhnyov! Pardon me for having troubled you.'

'Oh, not at all!' said Lezhnyov, and he went away.

'Well, what do you say to that?' Darya Mihailovna asked of Rudin. 'I had heard he was eccentric, but really that was beyond everything!'

'His is the same disease as Pigasov's,' observed Rudin, 'the desire of being original. One affects to be a Mephistopheles—the other a cynic. In all that, there is much egoism, much vanity, but little truth, little love. Indeed, there is even calculation of a sort in it. A man puts on a mask of indifference and indolence so that some one will be sure to think. "Look at that man; what talents he has thrown away!" But if you come to look at him more attentively, there is no talent in him whatever.'

'*Et de deux!*' was Darya Mihailovna's comment. 'You are a terrible man at hitting people off. One can hide nothing from you.'

'Do you think so?' said Rudin.... 'However,' he continued, 'I ought not really to speak about Lezhnyov; I loved him, loved him as a friend... but afterwards, through various misunderstandings...'

'You quarrelled?'

'No. But we parted, and parted, it seems, for ever.'

'Ah, I noticed that the whole time of his visit you were not quite yourself.... But I am much indebted to you for this morning. I have spent my time extremely pleasantly. But one must know where to stop. I will let you go till lunch time and I will go and look after my business. My secretary, you saw him—Constantin, *c'est lui qui est mon secrétaire*—must be waiting for me by now. I commend him to you; he is an excellent, obliging young man, and quite enthusiastic about you. *Au revoir, cher* Dmitri Nikolaitch! How grateful I am to the baron for having made me acquainted with you!'

And Darya Mihailovna held out her hand to Rudin. He first pressed it, then raised it to his lips and went away to the drawing-room and from there to the terrace. On the terrace he met Natalya.

V

Darya Mihailovna's daughter, Natalya Alexyevna, at a first glance might fail to please. She had not yet had time to develop; she was thin, and dark, and stooped slightly. But her features were fine and regular, though too large for a girl of seventeen. Specially beautiful was her pure, smooth forehead above fine eyebrows, which seemed broken in the middle. She spoke little, but listened to others, and fixed her eyes on them as though she were forming her own conclusions. She would often stand with listless hands, motionless and deep in thought; her face at such moments showed that her mind was at work within.... A scarcely perceptible smile would suddenly appear on her lips and vanish again; then she would slowly raise her large dark eyes. '*Qu'avez-vous?*' Mlle. Boncourt would ask her, and then she would begin to scold her, saying that it was improper for a young girl to be absorbed and to appear absent-minded. But Natalya was not absent-minded; on the contrary, she studied diligently; she read and worked eagerly. Her feelings were strong and deep, but reserved; even as a child she seldom cried, and now she seldom even sighed and only grew slightly pale when anything distressed her. Her mother considered her a sensible, good sort of girl, calling her in a joke '*mon honnête homme de fille*' but had not a very high opinion of her intellectual abilities. 'My Natalya happily is cold,' she used to say, 'not like me—and it is better so. She will be happy.' Darya Mihailovna was mistaken. But few mothers understand their daughters.

Natalya loved Darya Mihailovna, but did not fully confide in her.

'You have nothing to hide from me,' Darya Mihailovna said to her once, 'or else you would be very reserved about it; you are rather a close little thing.'

Natalya looked her mother in the face and thought, 'Why shouldn't I be reserved?'

When Rudin met her on the terrace she was just going indoors with Mlle. Boncourt to put on her hat and go out into the garden. Her morning occupations were over. Natalya was not treated as a school-girl now. Mlle. Boncourt had not given her lessons in mythology and geography for a long while; but Natalya had every morning to read historical books, travels, or other instructive works with her. Darya Mihailovna selected them, ostensibly on a special system of her own. In reality she simply gave Natalya everything which the French bookseller forwarded her from Petersburg, except, of course, the novels of Dumas Fils and Co. These novels Darya Mihailovna read herself. Mlle. Boncourt looked specially severely and sourly through her spectacles when Natalya was reading historical books; according to the old French lady's ideas all history was filled with *impermissible* things, though for some reason or other of all the great men of antiquity she herself knew only one—Cambyses, and of modern times—Louis XIV. and Napoleon, whom she could not endure. But Natalya read books too, the existence of which Mlle. Boncourt did not suspect; she knew all Pushkin by heart.

Natalya flushed slightly at meeting Rudin.

'Are you going for a walk?' he asked her.

'Yes. We are going into the garden.'

'May I come with you?'

Natalya looked at Mlle. Boncourt

'*Mais certainement, monsieur; avec plaisir,*' said the old lady promptly.

Rudin took his hat and walked with them.

Natalya at first felt some awkwardness in walking side by side with Rudin on the same little path; afterwards she felt more at ease. He began to question her about her occupations and how she liked the country. She replied not without timidity, but without that hasty bashfulness which is so often taken for modesty. Her heart was beating.

'You are not bored in the country?' asked Rudin, taking her in with a sidelong glance.

'How can one be bored in the country? I am very glad we are here. I am very happy here.'

'You are happy—that is a great word. However, one can understand it; you are young.'

Rudin pronounced this last phrase rather strangely; either he envied Natalya or he was sorry for her.

'Yes! youth!' he continued, 'the whole aim of science is to reach consciously what is bestowed on youth for nothing.'

Natalya looked attentively at Rudin; she did not understand him.

'I have been talking all this morning with your mother,' he went on; 'she is an extraordinary woman. I understand why all our poets sought her friendship. Are you fond of poetry?' he added, after a pause.

'He is putting me through an examination,' thought Natalya, and aloud: 'Yes, I am very fond of it.'

'Poetry is the language of the gods. I love poems myself. But poetry is not only in poems; it is diffused everywhere, it is around us. Look at those trees, that sky—on all sides there is the breath of beauty, and of life, and where there is life and beauty, there is poetry also.'

'Let us sit down. Here on this bench,' he added. 'Here—so. I somehow fancy that when you are more used to me (and he looked her in the face with a smile) 'we shall be friends, you and I. What do you think?'

'He treats me like a school-girl,' Natalya reflected again, and, not knowing what to say, she asked him whether he intended to remain long in the country.

'All the summer and autumn, and perhaps the winter too. I am a very poor man, you know; my affairs are in confusion, and, besides, I am tired now of wandering from place to place. The time has come to rest.'

Natalya was surprised.

'Is it possible you feel that it is time for you to rest?' she asked him timidly.

Rudin turned so as to face Natalya.

'What do you mean by that?'

'I mean,' she replied in some embarrassment, 'that others may rest; but you... you ought to work, to try to be useful. Who, if not you——'

'I thank you for your flattering opinion,' Rudin interrupted her. 'To be useful... it is easy to say!' (He passed his hand over his face.) 'To be useful!' he repeated. 'Even if I had any firm conviction, how could I be useful?— even if I had faith in my own powers, where is one to find true, sympathetic souls?'

And Rudin waved his hand so hopelessly, and let his head sink so gloomily, that Natalya involuntarily asked herself, were those really his—those enthusiastic words full of the breath of hope, she had heard the evening before.

'But no,' he said, suddenly tossing back his lion-like mane, 'that is all folly, and you are right. I thank you, Natalya Alexyevna, I thank you truly.' (Natalya absolutely did not know what he was thanking her for.) 'Your single phrase has recalled to me my duty, has pointed out to me my path.... Yes, I must act. I must not bury my talent, if I have any; I must not squander my powers on talk alone—empty, profitless talk—on mere words,' and his words flowed in a stream. He spoke nobly, ardently, convincingly, of the sin of cowardice and indolence, of the necessity of action. He lavished reproaches on himself, maintained that to discuss beforehand what you mean to do is as unwise as to prick with a pin the swelling fruit, that it is only a vain waste of strength and sap. He declared that there was no noble idea which would not gain sympathy, that the only people who remained misunderstood were those who either did not know themselves what they wanted, or were not worthy to be understood. He spoke at length, and ended by once more thanking

Natalya Alexyevna, and utterly unexpectedly pressed her hand, exclaiming. 'You are a noble, generous creature!'

This outburst horrified Mlle. Boncourt, who in spite of her forty years' residence in Russia understood Russian with difficulty, and was only moved to admiration by the splendid rapidity and flow of words on Rudin's lips. In her eyes, however, he was something of the nature of a virtuoso or artist; and from people of that kind, according to her notions, it was impossible to demand a strict adherence to propriety.

She got up and drew her skirts with a jerk around her, observed to Natalya that it was time to go in, especially as M. Volinsoff (so she spoke of Volintsev) was to be there to lunch.

'And here he is,' she added, looking up one of the avenues which led to the house, and in fact Volintsev appeared not far off.

He came up with a hesitating step, greeted all of them from a distance, and with an expression of pain on his face he turned to Natalya and said:

'Oh, you are having a walk?'

'Yes,' answered Natalya, 'we were just going home.'

'Ah!' was Volintsev's reply. 'Well, let us go,' and they all walked towards the house.

'How is your sister?' Rudin inquired, in a specially cordial tone, of Volintsev. The evening before, too, he had been very gracious to him.

'Thank you; she is quite well. She will perhaps be here to-day.... I think you were discussing something when I came up?'

'Yes; I have had a conversation with Natalya Alexyevna. She said one thing to me which affected me strongly.'

Volintsev did not ask what the one thing was, and in profound silence they all returned to Darya Mihailovna's house.

Before dinner the party was again assembled in the drawing-room. Pigasov, however, did not come. Rudin was not at his best; he did nothing but press Pandalevsky to play Beethoven. Volintsev was silent and stared at the floor. Natalya did not leave her mother's side, and was at times lost in thought, and then bent over her work. Bassistoff did not take his eyes off Rudin, constantly on the alert for him to say something brilliant. About three hours were passed in this way rather monotonously. Alexandra Pavlovna did not come to dinner, and when they rose from table Volintsev at once ordered his carriage to be ready, and slipped away without saying good-bye to any one.

His heart was heavy. He had long loved Natalya, and was repeatedly resolving to make her an offer.... She was kindly disposed to him,—but her heart remained unmoved; he saw that clearly. He did not hope to inspire in her a tenderer sentiment, and was only waiting for the time when she should be perfectly at home with him and intimate with him. What could have disturbed him? what change had he noticed in these two days? Natalya had behaved to him exactly the same as before....

Whether it was that some idea had come upon him that he perhaps did not know Natalya's character at all—that she was more a stranger to him than he had thought,—or jealousy had begun to work in him, or he had some dim presentiment of ill... anyway, he suffered, though he tried to reason with himself.

When he came in to his sister's room, Lezhnyov was sitting with her.

'Why have you come back so early?' asked Alexandra Pavlovna.

'Oh! I was bored.'

'Was Rudin there?'

'Yes.'

Volintsev flung down his cap and sat down. Alexandra Pavlovna turned eagerly to him.

'Please, Serezha, help me to convince this obstinate man (she signified Lezhnyov) that Rudin is extraordinarily clever and eloquent.'

Volintsev muttered something.

'But I am not disputing at all with you,' Lezhnyov began. 'I have no doubt of the cleverness and eloquence of Mr. Rudin; I only say that I don't like him.'

'But have you seen him?' inquired Volintsev.

'I saw him this morning at Darya Mihallovna's. You know he is her first favourite now. The time will come when she will part with him—Pandalevsky is the only man she will never part with—but now he is supreme. I saw him, to be sure! He was sitting there,—and she showed me off to him, "see, my good friend, what queer fish we have here!" But I am not a prize horse, to be trotted out on show, so I took myself off.'

'But how did you come to be there?'

'About a boundary; but that was all nonsense; she simply wanted to have a look at my physiognomy. She's a fine lady,—that's explanation enough!'

'His superiority is what offends you—that's what it is!' began Alexandra Pavlovna warmly, 'that's what you can't forgive. But I am convinced that besides his cleverness he must have an excellent heart as well. You should see his eyes when he———'

"'Of purity exalted speaks,'" quoted Lezhnyov.

'You make me angry, and I shall cry. I am heartily sorry I did not go to Darya Mihailovna's, but stopped with you. You don't deserve it. Leave off teasing me,' she added, in an appealing voice, 'You had much better tell me about his youth.'

'Rudin's youth?'

'Yes, of course. Didn't you tell me you knew him well, and had known him a long time?'

Lezhnyov got up and walked up and down the room.

'Yes,' he began, 'I do know him well. You want me to tell you about his youth? Very well. He was born in T———, and was the son of a poor landowner, who died soon after. He was left alone with his mother. She was a very good woman, and she idolised him; she lived on nothing but oatmeal, and every penny she had she spent on him. He was educated in Moscow, first at the expense of some uncle, and afterwards, when he was grown up and fully fledged, at the expense of a rich prince whose favour he had courted— there, I beg your pardon, I won't do it again—with whom he had made friends. Then he went to the university. At the university I got to know him and we became intimate friends. I will tell you about our life in those days some other time, I can't now. Then he went abroad....'

Lezhnyov continued to walk up and down the room; Alexandra Pavlovna followed him with her eyes.

'While he was abroad,' he continued, 'Rudin wrote very rarely to his mother, and paid her altogether only one visit for ten days.... The old lady died without him, cared for by strangers; but up to her death she never took her eyes off his portrait. I went to see her when I was staying in T———. She was a kind and hospitable woman; she always used to feast me on cherry jam. She loved her Mitya devotedly. People of the Petchorin type tell us that we always love those who are least capable of feeling love themselves; but it's my idea that all mothers love their children especially when they are absent. Afterwards I met Rudin abroad. Then he was connected with a lady, one of our countrywomen, a bluestocking, no longer young, and plain, as a bluestocking is bound to be. He lived a good while with her, and at last threw her over— or no, I beg pardon,—she threw him over. It was then that I too threw him over. That's all.'

Lezhnyov ceased speaking, passed his hand over his brow, and dropped into a chair as if he were exhausted.

'Do you know, Mihailo Mihailitch,' began Alexandra Pavlovna, 'you are a spiteful person, I see; indeed you are no better than Pigasov. I am convinced that all you have told me is true, that you have not made up anything, and yet in what an unfavourable light you have put it all! The poor old mother, her devotion, her solitary death, and that lady—What does it all amount to? You know that it's easy to put the life of the best of men in such colours—and without adding anything, observe—that every one would be shocked! But that too is slander of a kind!'

Lezhnyov got up and again walked about the room.

'I did not want to shock you at all, Alexandra Pavlovna,' he brought out at last, 'I am not given to slander. However,' he added, after a moment's thought, 'in reality there is a foundation of fact in what you said. I did not mean to slander Rudin; but—who knows! very likely he has had time to change since those days—very possibly I am unjust to him.'

'Ah! you see. So promise me that you will renew your acquaintance with him, and will get to know him thoroughly and then report your final opinion of him to me.'

'As you please. But why are you so quiet, Sergei Pavlitch?'

Volintsev started and raised his head, as though he had just waked up.

'What can I say? I don't know him. Besides, my head aches to-day.'

'Yes, you look rather pale this evening,' remarked Alexandra Pavlovna; 'are you unwell?'

'My head aches,' repeated Volintsev, and he went away.

Alexandra Pavlovna and Lezhnyov looked after him, and exchanged glances, though they said nothing. What was passing in Volintsev's heart was no mystery to either of them.

VI

More than two months had passed; during the whole of that period Rudin had scarcely been away from Darya Mihailovna's house. She could not get on without him. To talk to him about herself and to listen to his eloquence became a necessity for her. He would have taken his leave on one occasion, on the ground that all his money was spent; she gave him five hundred roubles. He borrowed two hundred roubles more from Volintsev. Pigasov visited Darya Mihailovna much less frequently than before; Rudin crushed him by his presence. And indeed it was not only Pigasov who was conscious of an oppression.

'I don't like that prig,' Pigasov used to say, 'he expresses himself so affectedly like a hero of a romance. If he says "I," he stops in rapt admiration, "I, yes, I!" and the phrases he uses are all so drawn-out; if you sneeze, he will begin at once to explain to you exactly why you sneezed and did not cough. If he praises you, it's just as if he were creating you a prince. If he begins to abuse himself, he humbles himself into the dust—come, one thinks, he will never dare to face the light of day after that. Not a bit of it! It only cheers him up, as if he'd treated himself to a glass of grog.'

Pandalevsky was a little afraid of Rudin, and cautiously tried to win his favour. Volintsev had got on to curious terms with him. Rudin called him a knight-errant, and sang his praises to his face and behind his back; but Volintsev could not bring himself to like him and always felt an involuntary impatience and annoyance when Rudin devoted himself to enlarging on his good points in his presence. 'Is he making fun of me?' he thought, and he felt a throb of hatred in his heart. He tried to keep his feelings in check, but in vain; he was jealous of him on Natalya's account. And Rudin himself, though he always welcomed Volintsev with effusion, though he called him a knight-errant, and borrowed money from him, did not feel exactly friendly towards him. It would be difficult to define the feelings of these two men when they pressed each other's hands like friends and looked into each other's eyes.

Bassistoff continued to adore Rudin, and to hang on every word he uttered. Rudin paid him very little attention. Once he spent a whole morning with him, discussing the weightiest problems of life, and awakening his keenest enthusiasm, but afterwards he took no further notice of him. Evidently it was only a phrase when he said that he was seeking for pure and devoted souls. With Lezhnyov, who began to be a frequent visitor at the house, Rudin did not enter into discussion; he seemed even to avoid him. Lezhnyov, on his part, too, treated him coldly. He did not, however, report his final conclusions about him, which somewhat disquieted Alexandra Pavlovna. She was fascinated by Rudin, but she had confidence in Lezhnyov. Every one in Darya Mihailovna's house humoured Rudin's fancies; his slightest preferences were carried out. He determined the plans for the day. Not a single *partie de plaisir* was arranged without his co-operation.

He was not, however, very fond of any kind of impromptu excursion or picnic, and took part in them rather as grown-up people take part in children's games, with an air of kindly, but rather wearied, friendliness. He took interest in everything else, however. He discussed with Darya Mihailovna her plans for the estate, the education of her children, her domestic arrangements, and her affairs generally; he listened to her schemes, and was not bored by petty details, and, in his turn, proposed reforms and made suggestions. Darya Mihailovna agreed to them in words—and that was all. In matters of business she was really guided by the advice of her bailiff— an elderly, one-eyed Little Russian, a good-natured and crafty old rogue. 'What is old is fat, what is new is thin,' he used to say, with a quiet smile, winking his solitary eye.

Next to Darya Mihailovna, it was Natalya to whom Rudin used to talk most often and at most length. He used privately to give her books, to confide his plans to her, and to read her the first pages of the essays and other works he had in his mind. Natalya did not always fully grasp the significance of them.

But Rudin did not seem to care much about her understanding, so long as she listened to him. His intimacy with Natalya was not altogether pleasing to Darya Mihailovna. 'However,' she thought, 'let her chatter away with him in the country. She amuses him as a little girl now. There is no great harm in it, and, at any rate, it will improve her mind. At Petersburg I will soon put a stop to it.'

Darya Mihailovna was mistaken. Natalya did not chatter to Rudin like a school-girl; she eagerly drank in his words, she tried to penetrate to their full significance; she submitted her thoughts, her doubts to him; he became her leader, her guide. So far, it was only the brain that was stirred, but in the young the brain is not long stirred alone. What sweet moments Natalya passed when at times in the garden on the seat, in the transparent shade of the aspen tree, Rudin began to read Goethe's *Faust*, Hoffman, or Bettina's letters, or Novalis, constantly stopping and explaining what seemed obscure to her. Like almost all Russian girls, she spoke German badly, but she understood it well, and Rudin was thoroughly imbued with German poetry, German romanticism and philosophy, and he drew her after him into these forbidden lands. Unimagined splendours were revealed there to her earnest eyes from the pages of the book which Rudin held on his knee; a stream of divine visions, of new, illuminating ideas, seemed to flow in rhythmic music into her soul, and in her heart, moved with the high delight of noble feeling, slowly was kindled and fanned into a flame the holy spark of enthusiasm.

'Tell me, Dmitri Nikolaitch,' she began one day, sitting by the window at her embroidery-frame, 'shall you be in Petersburg in the winter?'

'I don't know,' replied Rudin, as he let the book he had been glancing through fall upon his knee; 'if I can find the means, I shall go.'

He spoke dejectedly; he felt tired, and had done nothing all day.

'I think you are sure to find the means.'

Rudin shook his head.

'You think so!'

And he looked away expressively.

Natalya was on the point of replying, but she checked herself.

'Look.' began Rudin, with a gesture towards the window, 'do you see that apple-tree? It is broken by the weight and abundance of its own fruit. True emblem of genius.'

'It is broken because it had no support,' replied Natalya.

'I understand you, Natalya Alexyevna, but it is not so easy for a man to find such a support.'

'I should think the sympathy of others... in any case isolation always....'

Natalya was rather confused, and flushed a little.

'And what will you do in the country in the winter?' she added hurriedly.

'What shall I do? I shall finish my larger essay—you know it—on "Tragedy in Life and in Art." I described to you the outline of it the day before yesterday, and shall send it to you.'

'And you will publish it?'

'No.'

'No? For whose sake will you work then?'

'And if it were for you?'

Natalya dropped her eyes.

'It would be far above me.'

'What, may I ask, is the subject of the essay?' Bassistoff inquired modestly. He was sitting a little distance away.

'"Tragedy in Life and in Art,"' repeated Rudin. 'Mr. Bassistoff too will read it. But I have not altogether settled on the fundamental motive. I have not so far worked out for myself the tragic significance of love.'

Rudin liked to talk of love, and frequently did so. At first, at the word 'love,' Mlle. Boncourt started, and pricked up her eyes like an old war-horse at the sound of the trumpet; but afterwards she had grown used to it, and now only pursed up her lips and took snuff at intervals.

'It seems to me,' said Natalya timidly, 'that the tragic in love is unrequited love.'

'Not at all!' replied Rudin; 'that is rather the comic side of love. ... The question must be put in an altogether different way... one must attack it more deeply.... Love!' he pursued, 'all is mystery in love; how it comes, how it develops, how it passes away. Sometimes it comes all at once, undoubting, glad as day; sometimes it smoulders like fire under ashes, and only bursts into a flame in the heart when all is over; sometimes it winds its way into the heart like a serpent, and suddenly slips out of it again.... Yes, yes; it is the great problem. But who does love in our days? Who is so bold as to love?'

And Rudin grew pensive.

'Why is it we have not seen Sergei Pavlitch for so long?' he asked suddenly.

Natalya blushed, and bent her head over her embroidery frame.

'I don't know,' she murmured.

'What a splendid, generous fellow he is!' Rudin declared, standing up. 'It is one of the best types of a Russian gentleman.'

Mlle. Boncourt gave him a sidelong look out of her little French eyes.

Rudin walked up and down the room.

'Have you noticed,' he began, turning sharply round on his heels, 'that on the oak—and the oak is a strong tree—the old leaves only fall off when the new leaves begin to grow?'

'Yes,' answered Natalya slowly, 'I have noticed it.'

'That is what happens to an old love in a strong heart; it is dead already, but still it holds its place; only another new love can drive it out.'

Natalya made no reply.

'What does that mean?' she was thinking.

Rudin stood still, tossed his hair back, and walked away.

Natalya went to her own room. She sat a long while on her little bed in perplexity, pondering over Rudin's last words. All at once she clasped her hands and began to weep bitterly. What she was weeping for—who can tell? She herself could not tell why her tears were falling so fast. She dried them; but they flowed afresh, like water from a long-pent-up source.

On this same day Alexandra Pavlovna had a conversation with Lezhnyov about Rudin. At first he bore all her attacks in silence; but at last she succeeded in rousing him into talk.

'I see,' she said to him, 'you dislike Dmitri Nikolaitch, as you did before. I purposely refrained from questioning you till now; but now you have had time to make up your mind whether there is any change in him, and I want to know why you don't like him.'

'Very well,' answered Lezhnyov with his habitual phlegm, 'since your patience is exhausted; only look here, don't get angry.'

'Come, begin, begin.'

'And let me have my say to the end.'

'Of course, of course; begin.'

'Very well,' said Lezhnyov, dropping lazily on to the sofa; 'I admit that I certainly don't like Rudin. He is a clever fellow.'

'I should think so.'

'He is a remarkably clever man, though in reality essentially shallow.'

'It's easy to say that.'

'Though essentially shallow,' repeated Lezhnyov; 'but there's no great harm in that; we are all shallow. I will not even quarrel with him for being a tyrant at heart, lazy, ill-informed!'

Alexandra Pavlovna clasped her hands.

'Rudin—ill-informed!' she cried.

'Ill-informed!' repeated Lezhnyov in precisely the same voice, 'that he likes to live at other people's expense, to cut a good figure, and so forth—all that's natural enough. But what's wrong is, that he is as cold as ice.'

'He cold! that fiery soul cold!' interrupted Alexandra Pavlovna.

'Yes, cold as ice, and he knows it, and pretends to be fiery. What's bad,' pursued Lezhnyov, gradually growing warm, 'he is playing a dangerous game—not dangerous for him, of course; he does not risk a farthing, not a straw on it—but others stake their soul.'

'Whom and what are you talking of? I don't understand you,' said Alexandra Pavlovna.

'What's bad, he isn't honest. He's a clever man, certainly; he ought to know the value of his own words, and he brings them out as if they were worth something to him. I don't dispute that he's a fine speaker, but not in the Russian style. And indeed, after all, fine speaking is pardonable in a boy, but at his years it is disgraceful to take pleasure in the sound of his own voice, and to show off!'

'I think, Mihailo Mihailitch, it's all the same for those who hear him, whether he is showing off or not.'

'Excuse me, Alexandra Pavlovna, it is not all the same. One man says a word to me and it thrills me all over, another may say the same thing, or something still finer—and I don't prick up my ears. Why is that?'

'*You* don't, perhaps,' put in Alexandra Pavlovna.

'I don't,' retorted Lezhnyov, 'though perhaps my ears are long enough. The point is, that Rudin's words seem to remain mere words, and never to pass into deeds—and meanwhile even words may trouble a young heart, may be the ruin of it.'

'But whom do you mean, Mihailo Mihailitch?'

Lezhnyov paused.

'Do you want to know whom I mean, Natalya Alexyevna?'

Alexandra Pavlovna was taken aback for a moment, but she began to smile the instant after.

'Really,' she began, 'what queer ideas you always have! Natalya is still a child; and besides, if there were anything in what you say, do you suppose Darya Mihailovna——'

'Darya Mihailovna is an egoist to begin with, and lives for herself; and then she is so convinced of her own skill in educating her children that it does not even enter her head to feel uneasy about them. Nonsense! how is it possible: she has but to give one nod, one majestic glance—and all is over, all is obedience again. That's what that lady imagines; she fancies herself a female Maecenas, a learned woman, and God knows what, but in fact she is nothing more than a silly, worldly old woman. But Natalya is not a baby; believe me, she thinks more, and more profoundly too, than you and I do. And that her true, passionate, ardent nature must fall in with an actor, a flirt like this! But of course that's in the natural order of things.'

'A flirt! Do you mean that he is a flirt?'

'Of course he is. And tell me yourself, Alexandra Pavlovna, what is his position in Darya Mihailovna's house? To be the idol, the oracle of the household, to meddle in the arrangements, all the gossip and petty trifles of the house—is that a dignified position for a man to be in?'

Alexandra Pavlovna looked at Lezhnyov in surprise.

'I don't know you, Mihailo Mihailitch,' she began to say. 'You are flushed and excited. I believe there must be something else hidden under this.'

'Oh, so that's it! Tell a woman the truth from conviction, and she will never rest easy till she has invented some petty outside cause quite beside the point which has made you speak in precisely that manner and no other.'

Alexandra Pavlovna began to get angry.

'Bravo, Monsieur Lezhnyov! You begin to be as bitter against women as Mr. Pigasov; but you may say what you like, penetrating as you are, it's hard for me to believe that you understand every one and everything. I think you are mistaken. According to your ideas, Rudin is a kind of Tartuffe.'

'No, the point is, that he is not even a Tartuffe. Tartuffe at least knew what he was aiming at; but this fellow, for all his cleverness——'

'Well, well, what of him? Finish your sentence, you unjust, horrid man!'

Lezhnyov got up.

'Listen, Alexandra Pavlovna,' he began, 'it is you who are unjust, not I. You are cross with me for my harsh criticism of Rudin; I have the right to speak harshly of him! I have paid dearly enough, perhaps, for that privilege. I know him well: I lived a long while with him. You remember I promised to tell you some time about our life at Moscow. It is clear that I must do so now. But will you have the patience to hear me out?'

'Tell me, tell me!'

'Very well, then.'

Lezhnyov began walking with measured steps about the room, coming to a standstill at times with his head bent.

'You know, perhaps,' he began, 'or perhaps you don't know, that I was left an orphan at an early age, and by the time I was seventeen I had no one in authority over me. I lived at my aunt's at Moscow, and did just as I liked. As a boy I was rather silly and conceited, and liked to brag and show off. After my entrance at the university I behaved like a regular schoolboy, and soon got into a scrape. I won't tell you about it; it's not worth while. But I told a lie about it, and rather a shameful lie. It all came out, and I was put to open shame. I lost my head and cried like a child. It happened at a friend's rooms before a lot of fellow-students. They all began to laugh at me, all except one student, who, observe, had been more indignant with me than any, so long as I had been obstinate and would not confess my deceit. He took pity on me, perhaps; anyway, he took me by the arm and led me away to his lodging.'

'Was that Rudin?' asked Alexandra Pavlovna.

'No, it was not Rudin... it was a man... he is dead now... he was an extraordinary man. His name was Pokorsky. To describe him in a few words is beyond my powers, but directly one begins to speak of him, one does not want to speak of any one else. He had a noble, pure heart, and an intelligence such as I have never met since. Pokorsky lived in a little, low-pitched room, in an attic of an old wooden house. He was very poor, and supported himself somehow by giving lessons. Sometimes he had not even a cup of tea to offer to his friends, and his only sofa was so shaky that it was like being on board ship. But in spite of these discomforts a great many people used to go to see him. Every one loved him; he drew all hearts to him. You would not believe what sweetness and happiness there was in sitting in his poor little room! It was in his room I met Rudin. He had already parted from his prince before then.'

'What was there so exceptional in this Pokorsky?' asked Alexandra Pavlovna.

'How can I tell you? Poetry and truth—that was what drew all of us to him. For all his clear, broad intellect he was as sweet and simple as a child. Even now I have his bright laugh ringing in my ears, and at the same time he

Burnt his midnight lamp

Before the holy and the true,

as a dear half-cracked fellow, the poet of our set, expressed it.'

'And how did he talk?' Alexandra Pavlovna questioned again.

'He talked well when he was in the mood, but not remarkably so. Rudin even then was twenty times as eloquent as he.'

Lezhnyov stood still and folded his arms.

'Pokorsky and Rudin were very unlike. There was more flash and brilliance about Rudin, more fluency, and perhaps more enthusiasm. He appeared far more gifted than Pokorsky, and yet all the while he was a poor creature by comparison. Rudin was excellent at developing any idea, he was capital in argument, but his ideas did not come from his own brain; he borrowed them from others, especially from Pokorsky. Pokorsky was quiet and soft—even weak in appearance—and he was fond of women to distraction, and fond of dissipation, and he would never take an insult from any one. Rudin seemed full of fire, and courage, and life, but at heart he was cold and almost a coward, until his vanity was touched, then he would not stop at anything. He always tried to get an ascendency over people, but he got it in the name of general principles and ideas, and certainly had a great influence over many. To tell the truth, no one loved him; I was the only one, perhaps, who was attached to him. They submitted to his yoke, but all were devoted to Pokorsky. Rudin never refused to argue and discuss with any one he met. He did not read very much, though far more anyway than Pokorsky and all the rest of us; besides, he had a well-arranged intellect, and a prodigious memory, and what an effect that has on young people! They must have generalisations, conclusions, incorrect if you like, perhaps, but still conclusions! A perfectly sincere man never suits them. Try to tell young people that you cannot give them the whole truth, and they will not listen to you. But you mustn't deceive them either. You want to half believe yourself that you are in possession of the truth. That was why Rudin had such a powerful effect on all of us. I told you just now, you know, that he had not read much, but he read philosophical books, and his brain was so constructed that he extracted at once from what he had read all the general principles, penetrated to the very root of the thing, and then made deductions from it in all directions—consecutive, brilliant, sound ideas, throwing up a wide horizon to the soul. Our set consisted then—it's only fair to say—of boys, and not well-informed boys. Philosophy, art, science, and even life itself were all mere words to us—ideas if you like, fascinating and magnificent ideas, but disconnected and isolated. The general connection of those ideas, the general principle of the universe we knew nothing of, and had had no contact with, though we discussed it vaguely, and tried to form an idea of it for ourselves. As we listened to Rudin, we felt for the first time as if we had grasped it at last, this general connection, as if a veil had been lifted at last! Even admitting he was not uttering an original thought—what of that! Order and harmony seemed to be established in all we knew; all that had been disconnected seemed to fall into a whole, to take shape and grow like a building before our eyes, all was full of light and inspiration everywhere.... Nothing remained meaningless and undesigned, in everything wise design and beauty seemed apparent, everything took a clear and yet mystic significance; every isolated event of life fell into harmony, and with a kind of holy awe and reverence and sweet emotion we felt ourselves to be, as it were, the living vessels of eternal truth, her instruments destined for some great... Doesn't it all seem very ridiculous to you?'

'Not the least!' replied Alexandra Pavlovna slowly; 'why should you think so? I don't altogether understand you, but I don't think it ridiculous.'

'We have had time to grow wiser since then, of course,' Lezhnyov continued, 'all that may seem childish to us now.... But, I repeat, we all owed a great deal to Rudin then. Pokorsky was incomparably nobler than he, no question about it; Pokorsky breathed fire and strength into all of us; but he was often depressed and silent. He was nervous and not robust; but when he did stretch his wings—good heavens!—what a flight! up to the very height of the blue heavens! And there was a great deal of pettiness in Rudin, handsome and stately as he was; he was a gossip, indeed, and he loved to have a hand in everything, arranging and explaining everything. His fussy activity was inexhaustible—he was a diplomatist by nature. I speak of him as I knew him then. But unluckily he has not altered. On the other hand, his ideals haven't altered at five-and-thirty! It's not every one who can say that of himself!'

'Sit down,' said Alexandra Pavlovna, 'why do you keep moving about like a pendulum?'

'I like it better,' answered Lezhnyov. 'Well, after I had come into Pokorsky's set, I may tell you, Alexandra Pavlovna, I was quite transformed; I grew humble and anxious to learn; I studied, and was happy and reverent—in a word, I felt just as though I had entered a holy temple. And really, when I recall our gatherings, upon my word there was much that was fine, even touching, in them. Imagine a party of five or six lads gathered together, one tallow candle burning. The tea was dreadful stuff, and the cake was stale, very stale; but you should have seen our faces, you should have heard our talk! Eyes were sparkling with enthusiasm, cheeks flushed, and hearts beating, while we talked of God, and truth, of the future of humanity, and poetry ... often what we said was absurd, and we were in ecstasies over nonsense; but what of that?... Pokorsky sat with crossed legs, his pale cheek on his hand, and his eyes seemed to shed light. Rudin stood in the middle of the room and spoke, spoke splendidly, for all the world like the young Demosthenes by the resounding sea; our poet, Subotin of the dishevelled locks, would now and then throw out some abrupt exclamation as though in his sleep, while Scheller, a student forty years old, the son of a German pastor, who had the reputation among us of a profound thinker, thanks to his eternal, inviolable silence, held his peace with more rapt solemnity than usual; even the lively Shtchitof, the Aristophanes of our reunions, was subdued and did no more than smile, while two or three novices listened with reverent transports.... And the night seemed to fly by on wings. It was already the grey morning when we separated, moved, happy, aspiring and sober (there was no question of wine among us at such times) with a kind of sweet weariness in our souls... and one even looked up at the stars with a kind of confidence, as though they had become nearer and more comprehensible. Ah! that was a glorious time, and I can't bear to believe that it was altogether wasted! And it was not wasted—not even for those whose lives were sordid afterwards. How often have I chanced to come across such old college friends! You would think the man had sunk altogether to the brute, but one had only to utter Pokorsky's name before him and every trace of noble feeling in him was stirred at once;

it was like uncorking a forgotten phial of fragrance in some dark and dirty room.'

Lezhnyov stopped; his colourless face was flushed.

'And what was the cause of your quarrel with Rudin?' said Alexandra Pavlovna, looking wonderingly at Lezhnyov.

'I did not quarrel with him, but I parted from him when I came to know him thoroughly abroad. But I might well have quarrelled with him in Moscow, he did me a bad turn there.'

'What was that?'

'It was like this. I—how can I tell you?—it does not accord very well with my appearance, but I was always much given to falling in love.'

'You?'

'Yes, I was indeed. That's a curious idea, isn't it? But, anyway, it was so. Well, so I fell in love in those days with a very pretty young girl.... But why do you look at me like that? I could tell you something about myself a great deal more extraordinary than that!'

'And what is that something, if I may know?'

'Oh, just this. In those Moscow days I used to have a tryst at nights—with whom, would you imagine? with a young lime-tree at the bottom of my garden. I used to embrace its slender and graceful trunk, and I felt as though I were embracing all nature, and my heart melted and expanded as though it really were taking in the whole of nature. That's what I was then. And do you think, perhaps, I didn't write verses? Why, I even composed a whole drama in imitation of Manfred. Among the characters was a ghost with blood on his breast, and not his own blood, observe, but the blood of all humanity.... Yes, yes, you need not wonder at that. But I was beginning to tell you about my love affair. I made the acquaintance of a girl——'

'And you gave up your trysts with the lime-tree?' inquired Alexandra Pavlovna.

'Yes; I gave them up. This girl was a sweet, good creature, with clear, lively eyes and a ringing voice.'

'You give an excellent description of her,' commented Alexandra Pavlovna with a smile.

'You are such a severe critic,' retorted Lezhnyov. 'Well, this girl lived with her old father.... But I will not enter into details; I will only tell you that this girl was so kind-hearted, if you only asked her for half a cup of tea she would give it you brimming over! Two days after first meeting her I was wild over

- 66 -

her, and on the seventh day I could hold out no longer, and confessed it in full to Rudin. At that time I was completely under his influence, and his influence, I will tell you frankly, was beneficial in many things. He was the first person who did not treat me with contempt, but tried to lick me into shape. I loved Pokorsky passionately, and felt a kind of awe before his purity of soul, but I came closer to Rudin. When he heard about my love, he fell into an indescribable ecstasy, congratulated me, embraced me, and at once fell to disserting and enlarging upon all the dignity of my new position. I pricked up my ears.... Well, you know how he can talk. His words had an extraordinary effect on me. I at once assumed an amazing consequence in my own eyes, and I put on a serious exterior and left off laughing. I remember I used even to go about at that time with a kind of circumspection, as though I had a sacred chalice within me, full of a priceless liquid, which I was afraid of spilling over.... I was very happy, especially as I found favour in her eyes. Rudin wanted to make my beloved's acquaintance, and I myself almost insisted on presenting him.'

'Ah! I see, I see now what it is,' interrupted Alexandra Pavlovna. 'Rudin cut you out with your charmer, and you have never been able to forgive him.... I am ready to take a wager I am right!'

'You would lose your wager, Alexandra Pavlovna; you are wrong. Rudin did not cut me out; he did not even try to cut me out; but, all the same, he put an end to my happiness, though, looking at it in cool blood, I am ready to thank him for it now. But I nearly went out of my mind at the time. Rudin did not in the least wish to injure me—quite the contrary! But through his cursed habit of pinning every emotion—his own and other people's—with a phrase, as one pins butterflies in a case, he set to making clear to ourselves our relations to one another, and how we ought to treat each other, and arbitrarily compelled us to take stock of our feelings and ideas, praised us and blamed us, even entered into a correspondence with us—fancy! Well, he succeeded in completely disconcerting us! I should hardly, even then, have married the young lady (I had so much sense still left), but, at least, we might have spent some months happily a *la Paul et Virginie*; but now came strained relations, misunderstandings of every kind. It ended by Rudin, one fine morning, arriving at the conviction that it was his sacred duty as a friend to acquaint the old father with everything—and he did so.'

'Is it possible?' cried Alexandra Pavlovna.

'Yes, and did it with my consent, observe. That's where the wonder comes in!... I remember even now what a chaos my brain was in; everything was simply turning round—things looked as they do in a camera obscura—white seemed black and black white; falsehood was truth, and a whim was duty.... Ah! even now I feel shame at the recollection of it! Rudin—he never flagged—not a bit of it! He soared through all sorts of misunderstandings and perplexities, like a swallow over a pond.'

'And so you parted from the girl?' asked Alexandra Pavlovna, naively bending her head on one side, and raising her eyebrows.

'We parted—and it was a horrible parting—outrageously awkward and public, quite unnecessarily public.... I wept myself, and she wept, and I don't know what passed.... It seemed as though a kind of Gordian knot had been tied. It had to be cut, but it was painful! However, everything in the world is ordered for the best. She has married an excellent man, and is well off now.'

'But confess, you have never been able to forgive Rudin, all the same,' Alexandra Pavlovna was beginning.

'Not at all!' interposed Lezhnyov, 'why, I cried like a child when he was going abroad. Still, to tell the truth, even then there was the germ in my heart. And when I met him later abroad... well, by that time I had grown older.... Rudin struck me in his true light.'

'What was it exactly you discovered in him?'

'Why, all I have been telling you the last hour. But enough of him. Perhaps everything will turn out all right. I only wanted to show you that, if I do judge him hardly, it is not because I don't know him. ... As far as concerns Natalya Alexyevna, I won't say any more, but you should observe your brother.'

'My brother! Why?'

'Why, look at him. Do you really notice nothing?'

Alexandra Pavlovna looked down.

'You are right,' she assented. 'Certainly—my brother—for some time he has not been himself.... But do you really think——'

'Hush! I think he is coming,' whispered Lezhnyov. 'But Natalya is not a child, believe me, though unluckily she is as inexperienced as a child. You will see, that girl will astonish us all.'

'In what way?'

'Oh! in this way.... Do you know it's precisely girls like that who drown themselves, take poison, and so forth? Don't be misled by her looking so calm. Her passions are strong, and her character—my goodness!'

'Come! I think you are indulging in a flight of fancy now. To a phlegmatic person like you, I suppose even I seem a volcano?'

'Oh, no!' answered Lezhnyov, with a smile. 'And as for character—you have no character at all, thank God!'

'What impertinence is that?'

'That? It's the highest compliment, believe me.'

Volintsev came in and looked suspiciously at Lezhnyov and his sister. He had grown thin of late. They both began to talk to him, but he scarcely smiled in response to their jests, and looked, as Pigasov once said of him, like a melancholy hare. But there has certainly never been a man in the world who, at some time in his life, has not looked worse than that. Volintsev felt that Natalya was drifting away from him, and with her it seemed as if the earth was giving way under his feet.

VII

The next day was Sunday, and Natalya got up late. The day before she had been very silent all day; she was secretly ashamed of her tears, and she slept very badly. Sitting half-dressed at her little piano, at times she played some chords, hardly audibly for fear of waking Mlle. Boncourt, and then let her forehead fall on the cold keys and remained a long while motionless. She kept thinking, not of Rudin himself, but of some word he had uttered, and she was wholly buried in her own thought. Sometimes she recollected Volintsev. She knew that he loved her. But her mind did not dwell on him more than an instant.... She felt a strange agitation. In the morning she dressed hurriedly and went down, and after saying good-morning to her mother, seized an opportunity and went out alone into the garden.... It was a hot day, bright and sunny in spite of occasional showers of rain. Slight vapoury clouds sailed smoothly over the clear sky, scarcely obscuring the sun, and at times a downpour of rain fell suddenly in sheets, and was as quickly over. The thickly falling drops, flashing like diamonds, fell swiftly with a kind of dull thud; the sunshine glistened through their sparkling drops; the grass, that had been rustling in the wind, was still, thirstily drinking in the moisture; the drenched trees were languidly shaking all their leaves; the birds were busily singing, and it was pleasant to hear their twittering chatter mingling with the fresh gurgle and murmur of the running rain-water. The dusty roads were steaming and slightly spotted by the smart strokes of the thick drops. Then the clouds passed over, a slight breeze began to stir, and the grass began to take tints of emerald and gold. The trees seemed more transparent with their wet leaves clinging together. A strong scent arose from all around.

The sky was almost cloudless again when Natalya came into the garden. It was full of sweetness and peace—that soothing, blissful peace in which the heart of man is stirred by a sweet languor of undefined desire and secret emotion.

Natalya walked along a long line of silver poplars beside the pond; suddenly, as if he had sprung out of the earth, Rudin stood before her. She was confused. He looked her in the face.

'You are alone?' he inquired.

'Yes, I am alone,' replied Natalya, 'but I was going back directly. It is time I was home.'

'I will go with you.'

And he walked along beside her.

'You seem melancholy,' he said.

'I—I was just going to say that I thought you were out of spirits.'

'Very likely—it is often so with me. It is more excusable in me than in you.'

'Why? Do you suppose I have nothing to be melancholy about?'

'At your age you ought to find happiness in life.'

Natalya walked some steps in silence.

'Dmitri Nikolaitch!' she said.

'Well?'

'Do you remember—the comparison you made yesterday—do you remember—of the oak?'

'Yes, I remember. Well?'

Natalya stole a look at Rudin.

'Why did you—what did you mean by that comparison?'

Rudin bent his head and fastened his eyes on the distance.

'Natalya Alexyevna!' he began with the intense and pregnant intonation peculiar to him, which always made the listener believe that Rudin was not expressing even the tenth part of what he held locked in his heart—'Natalya Alexyevna! you may have noticed that I speak little of my own past. There are some chords which I do not touch upon at all. My heart—who need know what has passed in it? To expose that to view has always seemed sacrilege to me. But with you I cast aside reserve; you win my confidence.... I cannot conceal from you that I too have loved and have suffered like all men.... When and how? it's useless to speak of that; but my heart has known much bliss and much pain....'

Rudin made a brief pause.

'What I said to you yesterday,' he went on, 'might be applied in a degree to me in my present position. But again it is useless to speak of this. That side of life is over for me now. What remains for me is a tedious and fatiguing journey along the parched and dusty road from point to point... When I shall arrive—whether I arrive at all—God knows.... Let us rather talk of you.'

'Can it be, Dmitri Nikolaitch,' Natalya interrupted him, 'you expect nothing from life?'

'Oh, no! I expect much, but not for myself.... Usefulness, the content that comes from activity, I shall never renounce; but I have renounced happiness. My hopes, my dreams, and my own happiness have nothing in common. Love'—(at this word he shrugged his shoulders)—'love is not for me; I am not worthy of it; a woman who loves has a right to demand the whole of a man, and I can never now give the whole of myself. Besides, it is for youth to win love; I am too old. How could I turn any one's head? God grant I keep my own head on my shoulders.'

'I understand,' said Natalya, 'that one who is bent on a lofty aim must not think of himself; but cannot a woman be capable of appreciating such a man? I should have thought, on the contrary, that a woman would be sooner repelled by an egoist.... All young men—the youth you speak of—all are egoists, they are all occupied only with themselves, even when they love. Believe me, a woman is not only able to value self-sacrifice; she can sacrifice herself.'

Natalya's cheeks were slightly flushed and her eyes shining. Before her friendship with Rudin she would never have succeeded in uttering such a long and ardent speech.

'You have heard my views on woman's mission more than once,' replied Rudin with a condescending smile. 'You know that I consider that Joan of Arc alone could have saved France.... but that's not the point. I wanted to speak of you. You are standing on the threshold of life.... To dwell on your future is both pleasant and not unprofitable.... Listen: you know I am your friend; I take almost a brother's interest in you. And so I hope you will not think my question indiscreet; tell me, is your heart so far quite untouched?'

Natalya grew hot all over and said nothing, Rudin stopped, and she stopped too.

'You are not angry with me?' he asked.

'No,' she answered, 'but I did not expect——'

'However,' he went on, 'you need not answer me. I know your secret.'

Natalya looked at him almost with dismay.

'Yes, yes, I know who has won your heart. And I must say that you could not have made a better choice. He is a splendid man; he knows how to value you; he has not been crushed by life—he is simple and pure-hearted in soul... he will make your happiness.'

'Of whom are you speaking, Dmitri Niklaitch?'

'Is it possible you don't understand? Of Volintsev, of course. What? isn't it true?'

Natalya turned a little away from Rudin. She was completely overwhelmed.

'Do you imagine he doesn't love you? Nonsense! he does not take his eyes off you, and follows every movement of yours; indeed, can love ever be concealed? And do not you yourself look on him with favour? So far as I can observe, your mother, too, likes him.... Your choice——'

'Dmitri Nikolaitch,' Natalya broke in, stretching out her hand in her confusion towards a bush near her, 'it is so difficult, really, for me to speak of this; but I assure you... you are mistaken.'

'I am mistaken!' repeated Rudin. 'I think not. I have not known you very long, but I already know you well. What is the meaning of the change I see in you? I see it clearly. Are you just the same as when I met you first, six weeks ago? No, Natalya Alexyevna, your heart is not free.'

'Perhaps not,' answered Natalya, hardly audibly, 'but all the same you are mistaken.'

'How is that?' asked Rudin.

'Let me go! don't question me!' replied Natalya, and with swift steps she turned towards the house.

She was frightened herself by the feelings of which she was suddenly conscious in herself.

Rudin overtook her and stopped her.

'Natalya Alexyevna,' he said, 'this conversation cannot end like this; it is too important for me too.... How am I to understand you?'

'Let me go!' repeated Natalya.

'Natalya Alexyevna, for mercy's sake!'

Rudin's face showed his agitation. He grew pale.

'You understand everything, you must understand me too!' said Natalya; she snatched away her hand and went on, not looking round.

'Only one word!' cried Rudin after her

She stood still, but did not turn round.

'You asked me what I meant by that comparison yesterday. Let me tell you, I don't want to deceive you. I spoke of myself, of my past,—and of you.'

'How? of me?'

'Yes, of you; I repeat, I will not deceive you. You know now what was the feeling, the new feeling I spoke of then.... Till to-day I should not have ventured...'

Natalya suddenly hid her face in her hands, and ran towards the house.

She was so distracted by the unexpected conclusion of her conversation with Rudin, that she ran past Volintsev without even noticing him. He was standing motionless with his back against a tree. He had arrived at the house a quarter of an hour before, and found Darya Mihailovna in the drawing-room; and after exchanging a few words got away unobserved and went in search of Natalya. Led by a lover's instinct, he went straight into the garden and came upon her and Rudin at the very instant when she snatched her hand away from him. Darkness seemed to fall upon his eyes. Gazing after Natalya, he left the tree and took two strides, not knowing whither or wherefore. Rudin saw him as he came up to him. Both looked each other in the face, bowed, and separated in silence.

'This won't be the end of it,' both were thinking.

Volintsev went to the very end of the garden. He felt sad and sick; a load lay on his heart, and his blood throbbed in sudden stabs at intervals. The rain began to fall a little again. Rudin turned into his own room. He, too, was disturbed; his thoughts were in a whirl. The trustful, unexpected contact of a young true heart is agitating for any one.

At table everything went somehow wrong. Natalya, pale all over, could scarcely sit in her place and did not raise her eyes. Volintsev sat as usual next her, and from time to time began to talk in a constrained way to her. It happened that Pigasov was dining at Darya Mihailovna's that day. He talked more than any one at table. Among other things he began to maintain that men, like dogs, can be divided into the short-tailed and the long-tailed. People are short-tailed, he said, either from birth or through their own fault. The short-tailed are in a sorry plight; nothing succeeds with them—they have no confidence in themselves. But the man who has a long furry tail is happy. He may be weaker and inferior to the short-tailed; but he believes in himself; he displays his tail and every one admires it. And this is a fit subject for wonder; the tail, of course, is a perfectly useless part of the body, you admit; of what use can a tail be? but all judge of their abilities by their tail. 'I myself,' he concluded with a sigh, 'belong to the number of the short-tailed, and what is most annoying, I cropped my tail myself.'

'By which you mean to say,' commented Rudin carelessly, 'what La Rochefoucauld said long before you: Believe in yourself and others will believe in you. Why the tail was brought in, I fail to understand.'

'Let every one,' Volintsev began sharply and with flashing eyes, 'let every one express himself according to his fancy. Talk of despotism! ... I consider there is none worse than the despotism of so-called clever men; confound them!'

Everyone was astonished at this outbreak from Volintsev; it was received in silence. Rudin tried to look at him, but he could not control his eyes, and turned away smiling without opening his lips.

'Aha! so you too have lost your tail!' thought Pigasov; and Natalya's heart sank in terror. Darya Mihailovna gave Volintsev a long puzzled stare and at last was the first to speak; she began to describe an extraordinary dog belonging to a minister So-and-So.

Volintsev went away soon after dinner. As he bade Natalya good-bye he could not resist saying to her:

'Why are you confused, as though you had done wrong? You cannot have done wrong to any one!'

Natalya did not understand at all, and could only gaze after him. Before tea Rudin went up to her, and bending over the table as though he were examining the papers, whispered:

'It is all like a dream, isn't it? I absolutely must see you alone—if only for a minute.' He turned to Mlle. Boncourt. 'Here,' he said to her, 'this is the article you were looking for,' and again bending towards Natalya, he added in a whisper, 'Try to be near the terrace in the lilac arbour about ten o'clock; I will wait for you.'

Pigasov was the hero of the evening. Rudin left him in possession of the field. He afforded Darya Mihailovna much entertainment; first he told a story of one of his neighbours who, having been henpecked by his wife for thirty years, had grown so womanish that one day in crossing a little puddle when Pigasov was present, he put out his hand and picked up the skirt of his coat, as women do with their petticoats. Then he turned to another gentleman who to begin with had been a freemason, then a hypochondriac, and then wanted to be a banker.

'How were you a freemason, Philip Stepanitch?' Pigasov asked him.

'You know how; I wore the nail of my little finger long.'

But what most diverted Darya Mihailovna was when Pigasov set off on a dissertation upon love, and maintained that even he had been sighed for, that one ardent German lady had even given him the nickname of her 'dainty little African' and her 'hoarse little crow.' Darya Mihailovna laughed, but Pigasov spoke the truth; he really was in a position to boast of his conquests. He maintained that nothing could be easier than to make any woman you chose fall in love with you; you only need repeat to her for ten days in succession that heaven is on her lips and bliss in her eyes, and that the rest of womankind are all simply rag-bags beside her; and on the eleventh day she will be ready to say herself that there is heaven on her lips and bliss in her eyes, and will be in love with you. Everything comes to pass in the world; so who knows, perhaps Pigasov was right?

At half-past nine Rudin was already in the arbour. The stars had come out in the pale, distant depths of the heaven; there was still a red glow where the sun had set, and there the horizon seemed brighter and clearer; a semi-circular moon shone golden through the black network of the weeping birch-tree. The other trees stood like grim giants, with thousands of chinks looking like eyes, or fell into compact masses of darkness. Not a leaf was stirring; the topmost branches of the lilacs and acacias seemed to stretch upwards into the warm air, as though listening for something. The house was a dark mass now; patches of red light showed where the long windows were lighted up. It was a soft and peaceful evening, but under this peace was felt the secret breath of passion.

Rudin stood, his arms folded on his breast, and listened with strained attention. His heart beat violently, and involuntarily he held his breath. At last he caught the sound of light, hurrying footsteps, and Natalya came into the arbour.

Rudin rushed up to her, and took her hands. They were cold as ice.

'Natalya Alexyevna!' he began, in an agitated whisper, 'I wanted to see you.... I could not wait till to-morrow. I must tell you what I did not suspect—what I did not realise even this morning. I love you!'

Natalya's hands trembled feebly in his.

'I love you!' he repeated, 'and how could I have deceived myself so long? How was it I did not guess long ago that I love you? And you? Natalya Alexyevna, tell me!'

Natalya could scarcely draw her breath.

'You see I have come here,' she uttered, at last.

'No, say that you love me!'

'I think—yes,' she whispered.

Rudin pressed her hands still more warmly, and tried to draw her to him.

Natalya looked quickly round.

'Let me go—I am frightened.... I think some one is listening to us.... For God's sake, be on your guard. Volintsev suspects.'

'Never mind him! You saw I did not even answer him to-day.... Ah, Natalya Alexyevna, how happy I am! Nothing shall sever us now!'

Natalya looked into his eyes.

'Let me go,' she whispered; 'it's time.'

'One instant,' began Rudin.

'No, let me go, let me go.'

'You seem afraid of me.'

'No, but it's time.'

'Repeat, then, at least once more.'...

'You say you are happy?' asked Natalya.

'I? No man in the world is happier than I am! Can you doubt it?'

Natalya lifted up her head. Very beautiful was her pale, noble, young face, transformed by passion, in the mysterious shadows of the arbour, in the faint light reflected from the evening sky.

'I tell you then,' she said, 'I will be yours.'

'Oh, my God!' cried Rudin.

But Natalya made her escape, and was gone.

Rudin stood still a little while, then walked slowly out of the arbour. The moon threw a light on his face; there was a smile on his lips.

'I am happy,' he uttered in a half whisper. 'Yes, I am happy,' he repeated, as though he wanted to convince himself.

He straightened his tall figure, shook back his locks, and walked quickly into the garden, with a happy gesture of his hands.

Meanwhile the bushes of the lilac arbour moved apart, and Pandalevsky appeared. He looked around warily, shook his head, pursed up his mouth, and said, significantly, 'So that's how it is. That must be brought to Darya Mihailovna's knowledge.' And he vanished.

VIII

On his return home, Volintsev was so gloomy and dejected, he gave his sister such listless answers, and so quickly locked himself up in his room, that she decided to send a messenger to Lezhnyov. She always had recourse to him in times of difficulty. Lezhnyov sent her word that he would come in the next day.

Volintsev was no more cheerful in the morning. After tea he was starting to superintend the work on the estate, but he stayed at home instead, lay on the sofa, and took up a book—a thing he did not often do. Volintsev had no taste for literature, and poetry simply alarmed him. 'This is as incomprehensible as poetry,' he used to say, and, in confirmation of his words, he used to quote the following lines from a Russian poet:—

'And till his gloomy lifetime's close

Nor reason nor experience proud

Will crush nor crumple Destiny's

Ensanguined forget-me-nots.'

Alexandra Pavlovna kept looking uneasily at her brother, but she did not worry him with questions. A carriage drew up at the steps.

'Ah!' she thought, 'Lezhnyov, thank goodness!'

A servant came in and announced the arrival of Rudin.

Volintsev flung his book on the floor, and raised his head. 'Who has come?' he asked.

'Rudin, Dmitri Nikolaitch,' repeated the man. Volintsev got up.

'Ask him in,' he said, 'and you, sister,' he added, turning to Alexandra Pavlovna, 'leave us alone.'

'But why?' she was beginning.

'I have a good reason,' he interrupted, passionately. 'I beg you to leave us.'

Rudin entered. Volintsev, standing in the middle of the room, received him with a chilly bow, without offering his hand.

'Confess you did not expect me,' began Rudin, and he laid his hat down by the window. His lips were slightly twitching. He was ill at ease, but tried to conceal his embarrassment.

'I did not expect you, certainly,' replied Volintsev, 'after yesterday. I should have more readily expected some one with a special message from you.'

'I understand what you mean,' said Rudin, taking a seat, 'and am very grateful for your frankness. It is far better so. I have come myself to you, as to a man of honour.'

'Cannot we dispense with compliments?' observed Volintsev.

'I want to explain to you why I have come.'

'We are acquainted; why should you not come? Besides, this is not the first time you have honoured me with a visit.'

'I came to you as one man of honour to another,' repeated Rudin, 'and I want now to appeal to your sense of justice.... I have complete confidence in you.'

'What is the matter?' said Volintsev, who all this time was still standing in his original position, staring sullenly at Rudin, and sometimes pulling the ends of his moustache.

'If you would kindly... I came here to make an explanation, certainly, but all the same it cannot be done off-hand.'

'Why not?'

'A third person is involved in this matter.'

'What third person?'

'Sergei Pavlitch, you understand me?'

'Dmitri Nikolaitch, I don't understand you in the least.'

'You prefer——'

'I prefer you should speak plainly!' broke in Volintsev.

He was beginning to be angry in earnest.

Rudin frowned.

'Permit... we are alone... I must tell you—though you certainly are aware of it already (Volintsev shrugged his shoulders impatiently)—I must tell you that I love Natalya Alexyevna, and I have the right to believe that she loves me.'

Volintsev turned white, but made no reply. He walked to the window and stood with his back turned.

'You understand, Sergei Pavlitch,' continued Rudin, 'that if I were not convinced...'

'Upon my word!' interrupted Volintsev, 'I don't doubt it in the least.... Well! so be it! Good luck to you! Only I wonder what the devil induced you to come with this news to me.... What have I to do with it? What is it to me whom you love, or who loves you? It simply passes my comprehension.'

Volintsev continued to stare out of the window. His voice sounded choked.

Rudin got up.

'I will tell you, Sergei Pavlitch, why I decided to come to you, why I did not even think I had the right to hide from you our—our mutual feelings. I have too profound an esteem for you—that is why I have come; I did not want... we both did not wish to play a part before you. Your feeling for Natalya Alexyevna was known to me.... Believe me, I have no illusions about myself; I know how little I deserve to supplant you in her heart, but if it was fated this should be, is it made any better by pretence, hypocrisy, and deceit? Is it any better to expose ourselves to misunderstandings, or even to the possibilities of such a scene as took place yesterday at dinner? Sergei Pavlitch, tell me yourself, is it?'

Volintsev folded his arms on his chest, as though he were trying to hold himself in.

'Sergei Pavlitch!' Rudin continued, 'I have given you pain, I feel it—but understand us—understand that we had no other means of proving our respect to you, of proving that we know how to value your honour and uprightness. Openness, complete openness with any other man would have been misplaced; but with you it took the form of duty. We are happy to think our secret is in your hands.'

Volintsev gave vent to a forced laugh.

'Many thanks for your confidence in me!' he exclaimed, 'though, pray observe, I neither wished to know your secret, nor to tell you mine, though you treat it as if it were your property. But excuse me, you speak as though for two. Does it follow I am to suppose that Natalya Alexyevna knows of your visit, and the object of it?'

Rudin was a little taken aback.

'No, I did not communicate my intention to Natalya Alexyevna; but I know she would share my views.'

'That's all very fine indeed,' Volintsev began after a short pause, drumming on the window pane with his fingers, 'though I must confess it would have been far better if you had had rather less respect for me. I don't care a hang for your respect, to tell you the truth; but what do you want of me now?'

'I want nothing—or—no! I want one thing; I want you not to regard me as treacherous or hypocritical, to understand me... I hope that now you cannot doubt of my sincerity... I want us, Sergei Pavlitch, to part as friends... you to give me your hand as you once did.'

And Rudin went up to Volintsev.

'Excuse me, my good sir,' said Volintsev, turning round and stepping back a few paces, 'I am ready to do full justice to your intentions, all that's very fine, I admit, very exalted, but we are simple people, we do not gild our gingerbread, we are not capable of following the flight of great minds like yours.... What you think sincere, we regard as impertinent and disingenuous and indiscreet.... What is clear and simple to you, is involved and obscure to us.... You boast of what we conceal.... How are we to understand you! Excuse me, I can neither regard you as a friend, nor will I give you my hand.... That is petty, perhaps, but I am only a petty person.'

Rudin took his hat from the window seat.

'Sergei Pavlitch!' he said sorrowfully, 'goodbye; I was mistaken in my expectations. My visit certainly was rather a strange one... but I had hoped that you... (Volintsev made a movement of impatience). ... Excuse me, I will say no more of this. Reflecting upon it all, I see indeed, you are right, you could not have behaved otherwise. Good-bye, and allow me, at least once more, for the last time, to assure you of the purity of my intentions.... I am convinced of your discretion.'

'That is too much!' cried Volintsev, shaking with anger, 'I never asked for your confidence; and so you have no right whatever to reckon on my discretion!'

Rudin was about to say something, but he only waved his hands, bowed and went away, and Volintsev flung himself on the sofa and turned his face to the wall.

'May I come in?' Alexandra Pavlovna's voice was heard saying at the door.

Volintsev did not answer at once, and stealthily passed his hand over his face. 'No, Sasha,' he said, in a slightly altered voice, 'wait a little longer.'

Half an hour later, Alexandra Pavlovna again came to the door.

'Mihailo Mihailitch is here,' she said, 'will you see him?'

'Yes,' answered Volintsev, 'let them show him up here.'

Lezhnyov came in.

'What, aren't you well?' he asked, seating himself in a chair near the sofa.

Volintsev raised himself, and, leaning on his elbow gazed a long, long while into his friend's face, and then repeated to him his whole conversation with Rudin word for word. He had never before given Lezhnyov a hint of his sentiments towards Natalya, though he guessed they were no secret to him.

'Well, brother, you have surprised me!' Lezhnyov said, as soon as Volintsev had finished his story. 'I expected many strange things from him, but this is——Still I can see him in it.'

'Upon my honour!' cried Volintsev, in great excitement, 'it is simply insolence! Why, I almost threw him out of the window. Did he want to boast to me or was he afraid? What was the object of it? How could he make up his mind to come to a man——?'

Volintsev clasped his hands over his head and was speechless.

'No, brother, that's not it,' replied Lezhnyov tranquilly; 'you won't believe me, but he really did it from a good motive. Yes, indeed. It was generous, do you see, and candid, to be sure, and it would offer an opportunity of speechifying and giving vent to his fine talk, and, of course, that's what he wants, what he can't live without. Ah! his tongue is his enemy. Though it's a good servant to him too.'

'With what solemnity he came in and talked, you can't imagine!'

'Well, he can't do anything without that. He buttons his great-coat as if he were fulfilling a sacred duty. I should like to put him on a desert island and look round a corner to see how he would behave there. And he discourses on simplicity!'

'But tell me, my dear fellow,' asked Volintsev, 'what is it, philosophy or what?'

'How can I tell you? On one side it is philosophy, I daresay, and on the other something altogether different. It is not right to put every folly down to philosophy.'

Volintsev looked at him.

'Wasn't he lying then, do you imagine?'

'No, my son, he wasn't lying. But, do you know, we've talked enough of this. Let's light our pipes and call Alexandra Pavlovna in here. It's easier to talk when she's with us and easier to be silent. She shall make us some tea.'

'Very well,' replied Volintsev. 'Sasha, come in,' he cried aloud.

Alexandra Pavlovna came in. He grasped her hand and pressed it warmly to his lips.

Rudin returned in a curious and mingled frame of mind. He was annoyed with himself, he reproached himself for his unpardonable precipitancy, his boyish impulsiveness. Some one has justly said: there is nothing more painful than the consciousness of having just done something stupid.

Rudin was devoured by regret.

'What evil genius drove me,' he muttered between his teeth, 'to call on that squire! What an idea it was! Only to expose myself to insolence!'

But in Darya Mihailovna's house something extraordinary had been happening. The lady herself did not appear the whole morning, and did not come in to dinner; she had a headache, declared Pandalevsky, the only person who had been admitted to her room. Natalya, too, Rudin scarcely got a glimpse of: she sat in her room with Mlle. Boncourt. When she met him at the dinner-table she looked at him so mournfully that his heart sank. Her face was changed as though a load of sorrow had descended upon her since the day before. Rudin began to be oppressed by a vague presentiment of trouble. In order to distract his mind in some way he occupied himself with Bassistoff, had much conversation with him, and found him an ardent, eager lad, full of enthusiastic hopes and still untarnished faith. In the evening Darya Mihailovna appeared for a couple of hours in the drawing-room. She was polite to Rudin, but kept him somehow at a distance, and smiled and frowned, talking through her nose, and in hints more than ever. Everything about her had the air of the society lady of the court. She had seemed of late rather cooler to Rudin. 'What is the secret of it?' he thought, with a sidelong look at her haughtily-lifted head.

He had not long to wait for the solution of the enigma. As he was returning at twelve o'clock at night to his room, along a dark corridor, some one suddenly thrust a note into his hand. He looked round; a girl was hurrying away in the distance, Natalya's maid, he fancied. He went into his room, dismissed the servant, tore open the letter, and read the following lines in Natalya's handwriting:—

'Come to-morrow at seven o'clock in the morning, not later, to Avduhin pond, beyond the oak copse. Any other time will be impossible. It will be our last meeting, all will be over, unless... Come. We must make our decision.— P.S. If I don't come, it will mean we shall not see each other again; then I will let you know.'

Rudin turned the letter over in his hands, musing upon it, then laid it under his pillow, undressed, and lay down. For a long while he could not get to sleep, and then he slept very lightly, and it was not yet five o'clock when he woke up.

IX

The Avduhin pond, near which Natalya had fixed the place of meeting, had long ceased to be a pond. Thirty years before it had burst through its banks and it had been given up since then. Only by the smooth flat surface of the hollow, once covered with slimy mud, and the traces of the banks, could one guess that it had been a pond. A farm-house had stood near it. It had long ago passed away. Two huge pine-trees preserved its memory; the wind was for ever droning and sullenly murmuring in their high gaunt green tops. There were mysterious tales among the people of a fearful crime supposed to have been committed under them; they used to tell, too, that not one of them would fall without bringing death to some one; that a third had once stood there, which had fallen in a storm and crushed a girl.

The whole place near the old pond was supposed to be haunted; it was a barren wilderness, dark and gloomy, even on a sunny day—it seemed darker and gloomier still from the old, old forest of dead and withered oak-trees which was near it. A few huge trees lifted their grey heads above the low undergrowth of bushes like weary giants. They were a sinister sight; it seemed as though wicked old men had met together bent on some evil design. A narrow path almost indistinguishable wandered beside it. No one went near the Avduhin pond without some urgent reason. Natalya intentionally chose this solitary place. It was not more than half-a-mile from Darya Mihailovna's house.

The sun had already risen some time when Rudin reached the Avduhin pond, but it was not a bright morning. Thick clouds of the colour of milk covered the whole sky, and were driven flying before the whistling, shrieking wind. Rudin began to walk up and down along the bank, which was covered with clinging burdocks and blackened nettles. He was not easy in his mind. These interviews, these new emotions had a charm for him, but they also troubled him, especially after the note of the night before. He felt that the end was drawing near, and was in secret perplexity of spirit, though none would have imagined it, seeing with what concentrated determination he folded his arms across his chest and looked around him. Pigasov had once said truly of him, that he was like a Chinese idol, his head was constantly overbalancing him. But with the head alone, however strong it may be, it is hard for a man to know even what is passing in himself.... Rudin, the clever, penetrating Rudin, was not capable of saying certainly whether he loved Natalya, whether he was suffering, and whether he would suffer at parting from her. Why then, since he had not the least disposition to play the Lovelace—one must do him that credit—had he turned the poor girl's head? Why was he awaiting her with a secret tremor? To this the only answer is that there are none so easily carried away as those who are without passion.

He walked on the bank, while Natalya was hurrying to him straight across country through the wet grass.

'Natalya Alexyevna, you'll get your feet wet!' said her maid Masha, scarcely able to keep up with her.

Natalya did not hear and ran on without looking round.

'Ah, supposing they've seen us!' cried Masha; 'indeed it's surprising how we got out of the house... and ma'mselle may wake up... It's a mercy it's not far.... Ah, the gentleman's waiting already,' she added, suddenly catching sight of Rudin's majestic figure, standing out picturesquely on the bank; 'but what does he want to stand on that mound for—he ought to have kept in the hollow.'

Natalya stopped.

'Wait here, Masha, by the pines,' she said, and went on to the pond.

Rudin went up to her; he stopped short in amazement. He had never seen such an expression on her face before. Her brows were contracted, her lips set, her eyes looked sternly straight before her.

'Dmitri Nikolaitch,' she began, 'we have no time to lose. I have come for five minutes. I must tell you that my mother knows everything. Mr. Pandalevsky saw us the day before yesterday, and he told her of our meeting. He was always mamma's spy. She called me in to her yesterday.'

'Good God!' cried Rudin, 'this is terrible.... What did your mother say?'

'She was not angry with me, she did not scold me, but she reproached me for my want of discretion.'

'That was all?'

'Yes, and she declared she would sooner see me dead than your wife!'

'Is it possible she said that?'

'Yes; and she said too that you yourself did not want to marry me at all, that you had only been flirting with me because you were bored, and that she had not expected this of you; but that she herself was to blame for having allowed me to see so much of you... that she relied on my good sense, that I had very much surprised her... and I don't remember now all she said to me.'

Natalya uttered all this in an even, almost expressionless voice.

'And you, Natalya Alexyevna, what did you answer?' asked Rudin.

'What did I answer?' repeated Natalya.... 'What do *you* intend to do now?'

'Good God, good God!' replied Rudin, 'it is cruel! So soon... such a sudden blow!... And is your mother in such indignation?'

'Yes, yes, she will not hear of you.'

'It is terrible! You mean there is no hope?'

'None.'

'Why should we be so unhappy! That abominable Pandalevsky!... You ask me, Natalya Alexyevna, what I intend to do? My head is going round—I cannot take in anything... I can feel nothing but my unhappiness... I am amazed that you can preserve such self-possession!'

'Do you think it is easy for me?' said Natalya.

Rudin began to walk along the bank. Natalya did not take her eyes off him.

'Your mother did not question you?' he said at last.

'She asked me whether I love you.'

'Well... and you?'

Natalya was silent a moment. 'I told the truth.'

Rudin took her hand.

'Always, in all things generous, noble-hearted! Oh, the heart of a girl—it's pure gold! But did your mother really declare her decision so absolutely on the impossibility of our marriage?'

'Yes, absolutely. I have told you already; she is convinced that you yourself don't think of marrying me.'

'Then she regards me as a traitor! What have I done to deserve it?' And Rudin clutched his head in his hands.

'Dmitri Nikolaitch!' said Natalya, 'we are losing our time. Remember I am seeing you for the last time. I came here not to weep and lament—you see I am not crying—I came for advice.'

'And what advice can I give you, Natalya Alexyevna?'

'What advice? You are a man; I am used to trusting to you, I shall trust you to the end. Tell me, what are your plans?'

'My plans.... Your mother certainly will turn me out of the house.'

'Perhaps. She told me yesterday that she must break off all acquaintance with you.... But you do not answer my question?'

'What question?'

'What do you think we must do now?'

'What we must do?' replied Rudin; 'of course submit.'

'Submit,' repeated Natalya slowly, and her lips turned white.

'Submit to destiny,' continued Rudin. 'What is to be done? I know very well how bitter it is, how painful, how unendurable. But consider yourself, Natalya Alexyevna; I am poor. It is true I could work; but even if I were a rich man, could you bear a violent separation from your family, your mother's anger?... No, Natalya Alexyevna; it is useless even to think of it. It is clear it was not fated for us to live together, and the happiness of which I dreamed is not for me!'

All at once Natalya hid her face in her hands and began to weep. Rudin went up to her.

'Natalya Alexyevna! dear Natalya!' he said with warmth, 'do not cry, for God's sake, do not torture me, be comforted.'

Natalya raised her head.

'You tell me to be comforted,' she began, and her eyes blazed through her tears; 'I am not weeping for what you suppose—I am not sad for that; I am sad because I have been deceived in you.... What! I come to you for counsel, and at such a moment!—and your first word is, submit! submit! So this is how you translate your talk of independence, of sacrifice, which...'

Her voice broke down.

'But, Natalya Alexyevna,' began Rudin in confusion, 'remember—I do not disown my words—only——'

'You asked me,' she continued with new force, 'what I answered my mother, when she declared she would sooner agree to my death than my marriage to you; I answered that I would sooner die than marry any other man... And you say, "Submit!" It must be that she is right; you must, through having nothing to do, through being bored, have been playing with me.'

'I swear to you, Natalya Alexyevna—I assure you,' maintained Rudin.

But she did not listen to him.

'Why did you not stop me? Why did you yourself—or did you not reckon upon obstacles? I am ashamed to speak of this—but I see it is all over now.'

'You must be calm, Natalya Alexyevna,' Rudin was beginning; 'we must think together what means——'

'You have so often talked of self-sacrifice,' she broke in, 'but do you know, if you had said to me to-day at once, "I love you, but I cannot marry you, I will not answer for the future, give me your hand and come with me"—do you know, I would have come with you; do you know, I would have risked everything? But there's all the difference between word and deed, and you were afraid now, just as you were afraid the day before yesterday at dinner of Volintsev.'

The colour rushed to Rudin's face. Natalya's unexpected energy had astounded him; but her last words wounded his vanity.

'You are too angry now, Natalya Alexyevna,' he began; 'you cannot realise how bitterly you wound me. I hope that in time you will do me justice; you will understand what it has cost me to renounce the happiness which you have said yourself would have laid upon me no obligations. Your peace is dearer to me than anything in the world, and I should have been the basest of men, if I could have taken advantage——'

'Perhaps, perhaps,' interrupted Natalya, 'perhaps you are right; I don't know what I am saying. But up to this time I believed in you, believed in every word you said.... For the future, pray keep a watch upon your words, do not fling them about at hazard. When I said to you, "I love you," I knew what that word meant; I was ready for everything.... Now I have only to thank you for a lesson—and to say good-bye.'

'Stop, for God's sake, Natalya Alexyevna, I beseech you. I do not deserve your contempt, I swear to you. Put yourself in my position. I am responsible for you and for myself. If I did not love you with the most devoted love— why, good God! I should have at once proposed you should run away with me.... Sooner or later your mother would forgive us—and then... But before thinking of my own happiness——'

He stopped. Natalya's eyes fastened directly upon him put him to confusion.

'You try to prove to me that you are an honourable man, Dmitri Nikolaitch,' she said. 'I do not doubt that. You are not capable of acting from calculation; but did I want to be convinced of that? did I come here for that?'

'I did not expect, Natalya Alexyevna——'

'Ah! you have said it at last! Yes, you did not expect all this—you did not know me. Do not be uneasy... you do not love me, and I will never force myself on any one.'

'I love you!' cried Rudin.

Natalya drew herself up.

'Perhaps; but how do you love me? Remember all your words, Dmitri Nikolaitch. You told me: "Without complete equality there is no love."... You are too exalted for me; I am no match for you.... I am punished as I deserve.

There are duties before you more worthy of you. I shall not forget this day....
Good-bye.'

'Natalya Alexyevna, are you going? Is it possible for us to part like this?'

He stretched out his hand to her. She stopped. His supplicating voice seemed to make her waver.

'No,' she uttered at last. 'I feel that something in me is broken. ... I came here, I have been talking to you as if it were in delirium; I must try to recollect. It must not be, you yourself said, it will not be. Good God, when I came out here, I mentally took a farewell of my home, of my past—and what? whom have I met here?—a coward... and how did you know I was not able to bear a separation from my family? "Your mother will not consent... It is terrible!" That was all I heard from you, that you, you, Rudin?—No! good-bye.... Ah! if you had loved me, I should have felt it now, at this moment.... No, no, goodbye!'

She turned swiftly and ran towards Masha, who had begun to be uneasy and had been making signs to her a long while.

'It is *you* who are afraid, not I!' cried Rudin after Natalya.

She paid no attention to him, and hastened homewards across the fields. She succeeded in getting back to her bedroom; but she had scarcely crossed the threshold when her strength failed her, and she fell senseless into Masha's arms.

But Rudin remained a long while still standing on the bank. At last he shivered, and with slow steps made his way to the little path and quietly walked along it. He was deeply ashamed... and wounded. 'What a girl!' he thought, 'at seventeen!... No, I did not know her!... She is a remarkable girl. What strength of will!... She is right; she deserves another love than what I felt for her. I felt for her?' he asked himself. 'Can it be I already feel no more love for her? So this is how it was all to end! What a pitiful wretch I was beside her!'

The slight rattle of a racing droshky made Rudin raise his head. Lezhnyov was driving to meet him with his invariable trotting pony. Rudin bowed to him without speaking, and as though struck with a sudden thought, turned out of the road and walked quickly in the direction of Darya Mihailovna's house.

Lezhnyov let him pass, looked after him, and after a moment's thought he too turned his horse's head round, and drove back to Volintsev's, where he had spent the night. He found him asleep, and giving orders he should not be waked, he sat down on the balcony to wait for some tea and smoked a pipe.

X

Volintsev got up at ten o'clock. When he heard that Lezhnyov was sitting in the balcony, he was much surprised, and sent to ask him to come to him.

'What has happened?' he asked him. 'I thought you meant to drive home?'

'Yes; I did mean to, but I met Rudin.... He was wandering about the country with such a distracted countenance. So I turned back at once.'

'You came back because you met Rudin?'

'That's to say,—to tell the truth, I don't know why I came back myself, I suppose because I was reminded of you; I wanted to be with you, and I have plenty of time before I need go home.'

Volintsev smiled bitterly.

'Yes; one cannot think of Rudin now without thinking of me.... Boy!' he cried harshly, 'bring us some tea.'

The friends began to drink tea. Lezhnyov talked of agricultural matters,—of a new method of roofing barns with paper....

Suddenly Volintsev leaped up from his chair and struck the table with such force that the cups and saucers rang.

'No!' he cried, 'I cannot bear this any longer! I will call out this witty fellow, and let him shoot me,—at least I will try to put a bullet through his learned brains!'

'What are you talking about? Upon my word!' grumbled Lezhnyov, 'how can you scream like that? I dropped my pipe.... What's the matter with you?'

'The matter is, that I can't hear his name and keep calm; it sets all my blood boiling!'

'Hush, my dear fellow, hush! aren't you ashamed?' rejoined Lezhnyov, picking up his pipe from the ground. 'Leave off! Let him alone!'

'He has insulted me,' pursued Volintsev, walking up and down the room. 'Yes! he has insulted me. You must admit that yourself. At first I was not sharp enough; he took me by surprise; and who could have expected this? But I will show him that he cannot make a fool of me. ... I will shoot him, the damned philosopher, like a partridge.'

'Much you will gain by that, indeed! I won't speak of your sister now. I can see you're in a passion... how could you think of your sister! But in relation to another individual—what! do you imagine, when you've killed the philosopher, you can improve your own chances?'

Volintsev flung himself into a chair.

'Then I must go away somewhere! For here my heart is simply being crushed by misery; only I can find no place to go.'

'Go away... that's another matter! That I am ready to agree to. And do you know what I should suggest? Let us go together—to the Caucasus, or simply to Little Russia to eat dumplings. That's a capital idea, my dear fellow!'

'Yes; but whom shall we leave my sister with?'

'And why should not Alexandra Pavlovna come with us? Upon my soul, it will be splendid. As for looking after her—yes, I'll undertake that! There will be no difficulty in getting anything we want: if she likes, I will arrange a serenade under her window every night; I will sprinkle the coachmen with *eau de cologne* and strew flowers along the roads. And we shall both be simply new men, my dear boy; we shall enjoy ourselves so, we shall come back so fat that we shall be proof against the darts of love!'

'You are always joking, Misha!'

'I'm not joking at all. It was a brilliant idea of yours.'

'No; nonsense!' Volintsev shouted again. 'I want to fight him, to fight him!...'

'Again! What a rage you are in!'

A servant entered with a letter in his hand.

'From whom?' asked Lezhnyov.

'From Rudin, Dmitri Nikolaitch. The Lasunsky's servant brought it.'

'From Rudin?' repeated Volintsev, 'to whom?'

'To you.'

'To me!... give it me!'

Volintsev seized the letter, quickly tore it open, and began to read. Lezhnyov watched him attentively; a strange, almost joyful amazement was expressed on Volintsev's face; he let his hands fall by his side.

'What is it?' asked Lezhnyov.

'Read it,' Volintsev said in a low voice, and handed him the letter.

Lezhnyov began to read. This is what Rudin wrote:

'SIR—

'I am going away from Darya Mihailovna's house to-day, and leaving it for ever. This will certainly be a surprise to you, especially after what passed yesterday. I cannot explain to you what exactly obliges me to act in this way; but it seems to me for some reason that I ought to let you know of my departure. You do not like me, and even regard me as a bad man. I do not intend to justify myself; time will justify me. In my opinion it is even undignified in a man and quite unprofitable to try to prove to a prejudiced man the injustice of his prejudice. Whoever wishes to understand me will not blame me, and as for any one who does not wish, or cannot do so,—his censure does not pain me. I was mistaken in you. In my eyes you remain as before a noble and honourable man, but I imagined you were able to be superior to the surroundings in which you were brought up. I was mistaken. What of that? It is not the first, nor will it be the last time. I repeat to you, I am going away. I wish you all happiness. Confess that this wish is completely disinterested, and I hope that now you will be happy. Perhaps in time you will change your opinion of me. Whether we shall ever meet again, I don't know, but in any case I remain your sincere well-wisher,

'D. R.

'P.S. The two hundred roubles I owe you I will send directly I reach my estate in T—— province. Also I beg you not to speak to Darya Mihailovna of this letter.

'P.P.S. One last, but important request more; since I am going away, I hope you will not allude before Natalya Alexyevna to my visit to you.'

'Well, what do you say to that?' asked Volintsev, directly Lezhnyov had finished the letter.

'What is one to say?' replied Lezhnyov, 'Cry "Allah! Allah!" like a Mussulman and sit gaping with astonishment—that's all one can do.... Well, a good riddance! But it's curious: you see he thought it his *duty* to write you this letter, and he came to see you from a sense of *duty*... these gentlemen find a duty at every step, some duty they owe... or some debt,' added Lezhnyov, pointing with a smile to the postscript.

'And what phrases he rounds off!' cried Volintsev. 'He was mistaken in me. He expected I would be superior to my surroundings. What a rigmarole! Good God! it's worse than poetry!'

Lezhnyov made no reply, but his eyes were smiling. Volintsev got up.

'I want to go to Darya Mihailovna's,' he announced. 'I want to find out what it all means.'

'Wait a little, my dear boy; give him time to get off. What's the good of running up against him again? He is to vanish, it seems. What more do you want? Better go and lie down and get a little sleep; you have been tossing about all night, I expect. But everything will be smooth for you.'

'What leads you to that conclusion?'

'Oh, I think so. There, go and have a nap; I will go and see your sister. I will keep her company.'

'I don't want to sleep in the least. What's the object of my going to bed? I had rather go out to the fields,' said Volintsev, putting on his out-of-door coat.

'Well, that's a good thing too. Go along, and look at the fields....'

And Lezhnyov betook himself to the apartments of Alexandra Pavlovna. He found her in the drawing-room. She welcomed him effusively. She was always pleased when he came; but her face still looked sorrowful. She was uneasy about Rudin's visit the day before.

'You have seen my brother?' she asked Lezhnyov. 'How is he to-day?'

'All right, he has gone to the fields.'

Alexandra Favlovna did not speak for a minute.

'Tell me, please,' she began, gazing earnestly at the hem of her pocket-handkerchief, 'don't you know why...'

'Rudin came here?' put in Lezhnyov. 'I know, he came to say good-bye.'

Alexandra Pavlovna lifted up her head.

'What, to say good-bye!'

'Yes. Haven't you heard? He is leaving Darya Mihailovna's.'

'He is leaving?'

'For ever; at least he says so.'

'But pray, how is one to explain it, after all?...'

'Oh, that's a different matter! To explain it is impossible, but it is so. Something must have happened with them. He pulled the string too tight—and it has snapped.'

'Mihailo Mihailitch!' began Alexandra Pavlovna, 'I don't understand; you are laughing at me, I think....'

'No indeed! I tell you he is going away, and he even let his friends know by letter. It's just as well, I daresay, from one point of view; but his departure has prevented one surprising enterprise from being carried out that I had begun to talk to your brother about.'

'What do you mean? What enterprise?'

'Why, I proposed to your brother that we should go on our travels, to distract his mind, and take you with us. To look after you especially I would take on myself....'

'That's capital!' cried Alexandra Pavlovna. 'I can fancy how you would look after me. Why, you would let me die of hunger.'

'You say so, Alexandra Pavlovna, because you don't know me. You think I am a perfect blockhead, a log; but do you know I am capable of melting like sugar, of spending whole days on my knees?'

'I should like to see that, I must say!'

Lezhnyov suddenly got up. 'Well, marry me, Alexandra Pavlovna, and you will see all that'

Alexandra Pavlovna blushed up to her ears.

'What did you say, Mihailo Mihailitch?' she murmured in confusion.

'I said what it has been for ever so long,' answered Lezhnyov, 'on the tip of my tongue to say a thousand times over. I have brought it out at last, and you must act as you think best. But I will go away now, so as not to be in your way. If you will be my wife... I will walk away... if you don't dislike the idea, you need only send to call me in; I shall understand....'

Alexandra Pavlovna tried to keep Lezhnyov, but he went quickly away, and going into the garden without his cap, he leaned on a little gate and began looking about him.

'Mihailo Mihailitch!' sounded the voice of a maid-servant behind him, 'please come in to my lady. She sent me to call you.'

Mihailo Mihailitch turned round, took the girl's head in both his hands, to her great astonishment, and kissed her on the forehead, then he went in to Alexandra Pavlovna.

XI

On returning home, directly after his meeting with Lezhnyov, Rudin shut himself up in his room, and wrote two letters; one to Volintsev (already known to the reader) and the other to Natalya. He sat a very long time over this second letter, crossed out and altered a great deal in it, and, copying it carefully on a fine sheet of note-paper, folded it up as small as possible, and put it in his pocket. With a look of pain on his face he paced several times up and down his room, sat down in the chair before the window, leaning on his arm; a tear slowly appeared upon his eyelashes. He got up, buttoned himself up, called a servant and told him to ask Darya Mihailovna if he could see her.

The man returned quickly, answering that Darya Mihailovna would be delighted to see him. Rudin went to her.

She received him in her study, as she had that first time, two months before. But now she was not alone; with her was sitting Pandalevsky, unassuming, fresh, neat, and agreeable as ever.

Darya Mihailovna met Rudin affably, and Rudin bowed affably to her; but at the first glance at the smiling faces of both, any one of even small experience would have understood that something of an unpleasant nature had passed between them, even if it had not been expressed. Rudin knew that Darya Mihailovna was angry with him. Darya Mihailovna suspected that he was now aware of all that had happened.

Pandalevsky's disclosure had greatly disturbed her. It touched on the worldly pride in her. Rudin, a poor man without rank, and so far without distinction, had presumed to make a secret appointment with her daughter—the daughter of Darya Mihailovna Lasunsky.

'Granting he is clever, he is a genius!' she said, 'what does that prove? Why, any one may hope to be my son-in-law after that?'

'For a long time I could not believe my eyes,' put in Pandalevsky. 'I am surprised at his not understanding his position!'

Darya Mihailovna was very much agitated, and Natalya suffered for it

She asked Rudin to sit down. He sat down, but not like the old Rudin, almost master of the house, not even like an old friend, but like a guest, and not even a very intimate guest. All this took place in a single instant... so water is suddenly transformed into solid ice.

'I have come to you, Darya Mihailovna,' began Rudin, 'to thank you for your hospitality. I have had some news to-day from my little estate, and it is absolutely necessary for me to set off there to-day.'

Darya Mihailovna looked attentively at Rudin.

'He has anticipated me; it must be because he has some suspicion,' she thought. 'He spares one a disagreeable explanation. So much the better. Ah! clever people for ever!'

'Really?' she replied aloud. 'Ah! how disappointing! Well, I suppose there's no help for it. I shall hope to see you this winter in Moscow. We shall soon be leaving here.'

'I don't know, Darya Mihailovna, whether I shall succeed in getting to Moscow, but, if I can manage it, I shall regard it as a duty to call on you.'

'Aha, my good sir!' Pandalevsky in his turn reflected; 'it's not long since you behaved like the master here, and now this is how you have to express yourself!'

'Then I suppose you have unsatisfactory news from your estate?' he articulated, with his customary ease.

'Yes,' replied Rudin drily.

'Some failure of crops, I suppose?'

'No; something else. Believe me, Darya Mihailovna,' added Rudin, 'I shall never forget the time I have spent in your house.'

'And I, Dmitri Nikolaitch, shall always look back upon our acquaintance with you with pleasure. When must you start?'

'To-day, after dinner.'

'So soon!... Well, I wish you a successful journey. But, if your affairs do not detain you, perhaps you will look us up again here.'

'I shall scarcely have time,' replied Rudin, getting up. 'Excuse me,' he added; 'I cannot at once repay you my debt, but directly I reach my place——'

'Nonsense, Dmitri Nikolaitch!' Darya Mihailovna cut him short. 'I wonder you're not ashamed to speak of it!... What o'clock is it?' she asked.

Pandalevsky drew a gold and enamel watch out of his waistcoat pocket, and looked at it carefully, bending his rosy cheek over his stiff, white collar.

'Thirty-three minutes past two,' he announced.

'It is time to dress,' observed Darya Mihailovna. 'Good-bye for the present, Dmitri Nikolaitch!'

Rudin got up. The whole conversation between him and Darya Mihailovna had a special character. In the same way actors repeat their parts, and diplomatic dignitaries interchange their carefully-worded phrases.

Rudin went away. He knew by now through experience that men and women of the world do not even break with a man who is of no further use to them, but simply let him drop, like a kid glove after a ball, like the paper that has wrapped up sweets, like an unsuccessful ticket for a lottery.

He packed quickly, and began to await with impatience the moment of his departure. Every one in the house was very much surprised to hear of his intentions; even the servants looked at him with a puzzled air. Bassistoff did not conceal his sorrow. Natalya evidently avoided Rudin. She tried not to meet his eyes. He succeeded, however, in slipping his note into her hand. After dinner Darya Mihailovna repeated once more that she hoped to see him before they left for Moscow, but Rudin made her no reply. Pandalevsky addressed him more frequently than any one. More than once Rudin felt a longing to fall upon him and give him a slap on his rosy, blooming face. Mlle. Boncourt often glanced at Rudin with a peculiarly stealthy expression in her eyes; in old setter dogs one may sometimes see the same expression.

'Aha!' she seemed to be saying to herself, 'so you're caught!'

At last six o'clock struck, and Rudin's carriage was brought to the door. He began to take a hurried farewell of all. He had a feeling of nausea at his heart. He had not expected to leave this house like this; it seemed as though they were turning him out. 'What a way to do it all! and what was the object of being in such a hurry? Still, it is better so.' That was what he was thinking as he bowed in all directions with a forced smile. For the last time he looked at Natalya, and his heart throbbed; her eyes were bent upon him in sad, reproachful farewell.

He ran quickly down the steps, and jumped into his carriage. Bassistoff had offered to accompany him to the next station, and he took his seat beside him.

'Do you remember,' began Rudin, directly the carriage had driven from the courtyard into the broad road bordered with fir-trees, 'do you remember what Don Quixote says to his squire when he is leaving the court of the duchess? "Freedom," he says, "my friend Sancho, is one of the most precious possessions of man, and happy is he to whom Heaven has given a bit of bread, and who need not be indebted to any one!" What Don Quixote felt then, I feel now.... God grant, my dear Bassistoff, that you too may some day experience this feeling!'

Bassistoff pressed Rudin's hand, and the honest boy's heart beat violently with emotion. Till they reached the station Rudin spoke of the dignity of man, of the meaning of true independence. He spoke nobly, fervently, and justly, and when the moment of separation had come, Bassistoff could not refrain from throwing himself on his neck and sobbing. Rudin himself shed tears too, but he was not weeping because he was parting from Bassistoff. His tears were the tears of wounded vanity.

Natalya had gone to her own room, and there she read Rudin's letter.

'Dear Natalya Alexyevna,' he wrote her, 'I have decided to depart. There is no other course open to me. I have decided to leave before I am told plainly to go. By my departure all difficulties will be put an end to, and there will be scarcely any one who will regret me. What else did I expect?... It is always so, but why am I writing to you?

'I am parting from you probably for ever, and it would be too painful to me to leave you with a worse recollection of me than I deserve. This is why I am writing to you. I do not want either to justify myself or to blame any one whatever except myself; I want, as far as possible, to explain myself.... The events of the last days have been so unexpected, so sudden....

'Our interview to-day will be a memorable lesson to me. Yes, you are right; I did not know you, and I thought I knew you! In the course of my life I have had to do with people of all kinds. I have known many women and young girls, but in you I met for the first time an absolutely true and upright soul. This was something I was not used to, and I did not know how to appreciate you fittingly. I felt an attraction to you from the first day of our acquaintance; you may have observed it. I spent with you hour after hour without learning to know you; I scarcely even tried to know you—and I could imagine that I loved you! For this sin I am punished now.

'Once before I loved a woman, and she loved me. My feeling for her was complex, like hers for me; but, as she was not simple herself, it was all the better for her. Truth was not told to me then, and now I did not recognise it when it was offered me.... I have recognised it at last, when it is too late.... What is past cannot be recalled.... Our lives might have become united, and they never will be united now. How can I prove to you that I might have loved you with real love—the love of the heart, not of the fancy—when I do not know myself whether I am capable of such love?

'Nature has given me much. I know it, and I will not disguise it from you through false modesty, especially now at a moment so bitter, so humiliating for me.... Yes, Nature has given me much, but I shall die without doing anything worthy of my powers, without leaving any trace behind me. All my wealth is dissipated idly; I do not see the fruits of the seeds I sow. I am wanting in something. I cannot say myself exactly what it is I am wanting in.... I am wanting, certainly, in something without which one cannot move men's hearts, or wholly win a woman's heart; and to sway men's minds alone is precarious, and an empire ever unprofitable. A strange, almost farcical fate is mine; I would devote myself—eagerly and wholly to some cause,—and I cannot devote myself. I shall end by sacrificing myself to some folly or other in which I shall not even believe.... Alas! at thirty-five to be still preparing for something!...

'I have never spoken so openly of myself to any one before—this is my confession.

'But enough of me. I should like to speak of you, to give you some advice; I can be no use to you further.... You are still young; but as long as you live, always follow the impulse of your heart, do not let it be subordinated to your mind or the mind of others. Believe me, the simpler, the narrower the circle in which life is passed the better; the great thing is not to open out new sides, but that all the phases of life should reach perfection in their own time. "Blessed is he who has been young in his youth." But I see that this advice applies far more to myself than to you.

'I confess, Natalya Alexyevna, I am very unhappy. I never deceived myself as to the nature of the feeling which I inspired in Darya Mihailovna; but I hoped I had found at least a temporary home.... Now I must take the chances of the rough world again. What will replace for me your conversation, your presence, your attentive and intelligent face?... I myself am to blame; but admit that fate seems to have designed a jest at my expense. A week ago I did not even myself suspect that I loved you. The day before yesterday, that evening in the garden, I for the first time heard from your lips,... but why remind you of what you said then? and now I am going away to-day. I am going away disgraced, after a cruel explanation with you, carrying with me no hope.... And you do not know yet to what a degree I am to blame as regards you... I have such a foolish lack of reserve, such a weak habit of confiding. But why speak of this? I am leaving you for ever!'

(Here Rudin had related to Natalya his visit to Volintsev, but on second thoughts he erased all that part, and added the second postscript to his letter to Volintsev.)

'I remain alone upon earth to devote myself, as you said to me this morning with bitter irony, to other interests more congenial to me. Alas! if I could really devote myself to these interests, if I could at last conquer my inertia.... But no! I shall remain to the end the incomplete creature I have always been.... The first obstacle, ... and I collapse entirely; what has passed with you has shown me that. If I had but sacrificed my love to my future work, to my vocation; but I simply was afraid of the responsibility that had fallen upon me, and therefore I am, truly, unworthy of you. I do not deserve that you should be torn out of your sphere for me.... And indeed all this, perhaps, is for the best. I shall perhaps be the stronger and the purer for this experience.

'I wish you all happiness. Farewell! Think sometimes of me. I hope that you may still hear of me.

'RUDIN.'

Natalya let Rudin's letter drop on to her lap, and sat a long time motionless, her eyes fixed on the ground. This letter proved to her clearer than all possible arguments that she had been right, when in the morning, at her parting with Rudin, she had involuntarily cried out that he did not love her! But that made things no easier for her. She sat perfectly still; it seemed as though waves of darkness without a ray of light had closed over her head, and she had gone down cold and dumb to the depths. The first disillusionment is painful for every one; but for a sincere heart, averse to self-deception and innocent of frivolity or exaggeration, it is almost unendurable. Natalya remembered her childhood, how, when walking in the evening, she always tried to go in the direction of the setting sun, where there was light in the sky, and not toward the darkened half of the heavens. Life now stood in darkness before her, and she had turned her back on the light for ever....

Tears started into Natalya's eyes. Tears do not always bring relief. They are comforting and salutary when, after being long pent up in the breast, they flow at last—at first with violence, and then more easily, more softly; the dumb agony of sorrow is over with the tears. ... But there are cold tears, tears that flow sparingly, wrung out drop by drop from the heart by the immovable, weary weight of pain laid upon it: they are not comforting, and bring no relief. Poverty weeps such tears; and the man has not yet been unhappy who has not shed them. Natalya knew them on that day.

Two hours passed. Natalya pulled herself together, got up, wiped her eyes, and, lighting a candle, she burnt Rudin's letter in the flame, and threw the ash out of window. Then she opened Pushkin at random, and read the first lines that met her. (She often made it her oracle in this way.) This is what she saw:

When he has known its pang, for him

The torturing ghost of days that are no more,

For him no more illusion, but remorse

And memory's serpent gnawing at his heart.'

She stopped, and with a cold smile looked at herself in the glass, slightly nodded her head, and went down to the drawing-room.

Darya Mihailovna, directly she saw her, called her into her study, made her sit near her, and caressingly stroked her cheek. Meanwhile she gazed attentively, almost with curiosity, into her eyes. Darya Mihailovna was secretly perplexed; for the first time it struck her that she did not really understand her daughter. When she had heard from Pandalevsky of her meeting with Rudin, she was not so much displeased as amazed that her sensible Natalya could resolve upon such a step. But when she had sent for her, and fell to upbraiding her—not at all as one would have expected from a lady of European renown, but with loud and vulgar abuse—Natalya's firm replies, and the resolution of her looks and movements, had confused and even intimidated her.

Rudin's sudden, and wholly unexplained, departure had taken a great load off her heart, but she had expected tears, and hysterics.... Natalya's outward composure threw her out of her reckoning again.

'Well, child,' began Darya Mihailovna, 'how are you to-day?' Natalya looked at her mother. 'He is gone, you see... your hero. Do you know why he decided on going so quickly?'

'Mamma!' said Natalya in a low voice, 'I give you my word, if you will not mention him, you shall never hear his name from me.'

'Then you acknowledge how wrongly you behaved to me?'

Natalya looked down and repeated:

'You shall never hear his name from me.'

'Well, well,' answered Darya Mihailovna with a smile, 'I believe you. But the day before yesterday, do you remember how—There, we will pass that over. It is all over and buried and forgotten. Isn't it? Come, I know you again now; but I was altogether puzzled then. There, kiss me like a sensible girl!'

Natalya lifted Darya Mihailovna's hand to her lips, and Darya Mihailovna kissed her stooping head.

'Always listen to my advice. Do not forget that you are a Lasunsky and my daughter,' she added, 'and you will be happy. And now you may go.'

Natalya went away in silence. Darya Mihailovna looked after her and thought: 'She is like me—she too will let herself be carried away by her feelings; *mais ella aura moins d'abandon.*' And Darya Mihailovna fell to musing over memories of the past... of the distant past.

Then she summoned Mlle. Boncourt and remained a long while closeted with her.

When she had dismissed her she sent for Pandalevsky. She wanted at all hazards to discover the real cause of Rudin's departure... but Pandalevsky succeeded in completely satisfying her. It was what he was there for.

The next day Volintsev and his sister came to dinner. Darya Mihailovna was always very affable to him, but this time she was especially cordial to him.

Natalya felt unbearably miserable; but Volintsev was so respectful, and addressed her so timidly, that she could not but be grateful to him in her heart. The day passed quietly, rather tediously, but all felt as they separated that they had fallen back into the old order of things; and that means much, very much.

Yes, all had fallen back into their old order—all except Natalya. When at last she was able to be alone, she dragged herself with difficulty into her bed, and, weary and worn out, fell with her face on the pillow. Life seemed so cruel, so hateful, and so sordid, she was so ashamed of herself, her love, and her sorrow, that at that moment she would have been glad to die.... There were many sorrowful days in store for her, and sleepless nights and torturing emotions; but she was young—life had scarcely begun for her, and sooner or later life asserts its claims. Whatever blow has fallen on a man, he must—forgive the coarseness of the expression—eat that day or at least the next, and that is the first step to consolation.

Natalya suffered terribly, she suffered for the first time.... But the first sorrow, like first love, does not come again—and thank God for it!

XII

About two years had passed. The first days of May had come. Alexandra Pavlovna, no longer Lipin but Lezhnyov, was sitting on the balcony of her house; she had been married to Mihailo Mihailitch for more than a year. She was as charming as ever, and had only grown a little stouter of late. In front of the balcony, from which there were steps leading into the garden, a nurse was walking about carrying a rosy-cheeked baby in her arms, in a white cloak, with a white cap on his head. Alexandra Pavlovna kept her eyes constantly on him. The baby did not cry, but sucked his thumb gravely and looked about him. He was already showing himself a worthy son of Mihailo Mihailitch.

On the balcony, near Alexandra Pavlovna, was sitting our old friend, Pigasov. He had grown noticeably greyer since we parted from him, and was bent and thin, and he lisped when he spoke; one of his front teeth had gone; and this lisp gave still greater asperity to his words.... His spitefulness had not decreased with years, but his sallies were less lively, and he more frequently repeated himself. Mihailo Mihailitch was not at home; they were expecting him in to tea. The sun had already set. Where it had gone down, a streak of pale gold and of lemon colour stretched across the distant horizon; on the opposite quarter of the sky was a stretch of dove-colour below and crimson lilac above. Light clouds seemed melting away overhead. There was every promise of prolonged fine weather.

Suddenly Pigasov burst out laughing.

'What is it, African Semenitch?' inquired Alexandra Pavlovna.

'Oh, yesterday I heard a peasant say to his wife—she had been chattering away—"don't squeak!" I liked that immensely. And after all, what can a woman talk about? I never, you know, speak of present company. Our ancestors were wiser than we. The beauty in their stories always sits at the window with a star on her brow and never utters a syllable. That's how it ought to be. Think of it! the day before yesterday, our marshal's wife—she might have sent a pistol-shot into my head!—says to me she doesn't like my tendencies! Tendencies! Come, wouldn't it be better for her and for every one if by some beneficent ordinance of nature she were suddenly deprived of the use of her tongue?'

'Oh, you are always like that, African Semenitch; you are always attacking us poor... Do you know it's a misfortune of a sort, really? I am sorry for you.'

'A misfortune! Why do you say that? To begin with, in my opinion, there are only three misfortunes: to live in winter in cold lodgings, in summer to wear tight shoes, and to spend the night in a room where a baby cries whom you can't get rid of with Persian powder; and secondly, I am now the most peaceable of men. Why, I'm a model! You know how properly I behave!'

'Fine behaviour, indeed! Only yesterday Elena Antonovna complained to me of you.'

'Well! And what did she tell you, if I may know?'

'She told me that for one whole morning you would make no reply to all her questions but "what? what?" and always in the same squeaking voice.'

Pigasov laughed.

'But that was a happy idea, you'll allow, Alexandra Pavlovna, eh?'

'Admirable, indeed! Can you really have behaved so rudely to a lady, African Semenitch?'

'What! Do you regard Elena Antonovna as a lady?'

'What do you regard her as?'

'A drum, upon my word, an ordinary drum such as they beat with sticks.'

'Oh,' interrupted Alexandra Pavlovna, anxious to change the conversation, 'they tell me one may congratulate you.'

'Upon what?'

'The end of your lawsuit. The Glinovsky meadows are yours.'

'Yes, they are mine,' replied Pigasov gloomily.

'You have been trying to gain this so many years, and now you seem discontented.'

'I assure you, Alexandra Pavlovna,' said Pigasov slowly, 'nothing can be worse and more injurious than good-fortune that comes too late. It cannot give you pleasure in any way, and it deprives you of the right—the precious right—of complaining and cursing Providence. Yes, madam, it's a cruel and insulting trick—belated fortune.'

Alexandra Pavlovna only shrugged her shoulders.

'Nurse,' she began, 'I think it's time to put Misha to bed. Give him to me.'

While Alexandra Pavlovna busied herself with her son, Pigasov walked off muttering to the other corner of the balcony.

Suddenly, not far off on the road that ran the length of the garden, Mihailo Mihailitch made his appearance driving his racing droshky. Two huge house-dogs ran before the horse, one yellow, the other grey, both only lately obtained. They incessantly quarrelled, and were inseparable companions. An old pug-dog came out of the gate to meet them. He opened his mouth as if he were going to bark, but ended by yawning and turning back again with a friendly wag of the tail.

'Look here, Sasha,' cried Lezhnyov, from the distance, to his wife, 'whom I am bringing you.'

Alexandra Pavlovna did not at once recognise the man who was sitting behind her husband's back.

'Ah! Mr. Bassistoff!' she cried at last.

'It's he,' answered Lezhnyov; 'and he has brought such glorious news. Wait a minute, you shall know directly.'

And he drove into the courtyard.

Some minutes later he came with Bassistoff into the balcony.

'Hurrah!' he cried, embracing his wife, 'Serezha is going to be married.'

'To whom?' asked Alexandra Pavlovna, much agitated.

'To Natalya, of course. Our friend has brought the news from Moscow, and there is a letter for you.'

'Do you hear, Misha,' he went on, snatching his son into his arms, 'your uncle's going to be married? What criminal indifference! he only blinks his eyes!'

'He is sleepy,' remarked the nurse.

'Yes,' said Bassistoff, going up to Alexandra Pavlovna, 'I have come to-day from Moscow on business for Darya Mihailovna—to go over the accounts on the estate. And here is the letter.'

Alexandra Pavlovna opened her brother's letter in haste. It consisted of a few lines only. In the first transport of joy he informed his sister that he had made Natalya an offer, and received her consent and Darya Mihailovna's; and he promised to write more by the next post, and sent embraces and kisses to all. It was clear he was writing in a state of delirium.

Tea was served, Bassistoff sat down. Questions were showered upon him. Every one, even Pigasov, was delighted at the news he had brought.

'Tell me, please,' said Lezhnyov among the rest, 'rumours reached us of a certain Mr. Kortchagin. That was all nonsense, I suppose?'

Kortchagin was a handsome young man, a society lion, excessively conceited and important; he behaved with extraordinary dignity, just as if he had not been a living man, but his own statue set up by public subscription.

'Well, no, not altogether nonsense,' replied Bassistoff with a smile; 'Darya Mihailovna was very favourable to him; but Natalya Alexyevna would not even hear of him.'

'I know him,' put in Pigasov, 'he's a double dummy, a noisy dummy, if you like! If all people were like that, it would need a large sum of money to induce one to consent to live—upon my word!'

'Very likely,' answered Bassistoff; 'but he plays a leading part in society.'

'Well, never mind him!' cried Alexandra Pavlovna. 'Peace be with him! Ah! how glad I am for my brother! And Natalya, is she bright and happy?'

'Yes. She is quiet, as she always is. You know her—but she seems contented.'

The evening was spent in friendly and lively talk. They sat down to supper.

'Oh, by the way,' inquired Lezhnyov of Bassistoff, as he poured him out some Lafitte, 'do you know where Rudin is?'

'I don't know for certain now. He came last winter to Moscow for a short time, and then went with a family to Simbirsk. I corresponded with him for some time; in his last letter he informed me he was leaving Simbirsk—he did not say where he was going—and since then I have heard nothing of him.'

'He is all right!' put in Pigasov. 'He is staying somewhere sermonising. That gentleman will always find two or three adherents everywhere, to listen to him open-mouthed and lend him money. You will see he will end by dying in some out-of-the-way corner in the arms of an old maid in a wig, who will believe he is the greatest genius in the world.'

'You speak very harshly of him,' remarked Bassistoff, in a displeased undertone.

'Not a bit harshly,' replied Pigasov; 'but perfectly fairly. In my opinion, he is simply nothing else than a sponge. I forgot to tell you,' he continued, turning to Lezhnyov, 'that I have made the acquaintance of that Terlahov, with whom Rudin travelled abroad. Yes! Yes! What he told me of him, you cannot imagine—it's simply screaming! It's a remarkable fact that all Rudin's friends and admirers become in time his enemies.'

'I beg you to except me from the number of such friends!' interposed Bassistoff warmly.

'Oh, you—that's a different thing! I was not speaking of you.'

'But what did Terlahov tell you?' asked Alexandra Pavlovna.

'Oh, he told me a great deal; there's no remembering it all. But the best of all was an anecdote of what happened to Rudin. As he was incessantly developing (these gentlemen always are developing; other people simply sleep and eat; but they manage their sleeping and eating in the intervals of development; isn't that it, Mr. Bassistoff?' Bassistoff made no reply.) 'And so, as he was continually developing, Rudin arrived at the conclusion, by means of philosophy, that he ought to fall in love. He began to look about for a sweetheart worthy of such an astonishing conclusion. Fortune smiled upon him. He made the acquaintance of a very pretty French dressmaker. The whole incident occurred in a German town on the Rhine, observe. He began to go and see her, to take her various books, to talk to her of Nature and Hegel. Can you fancy the position of the dressmaker? She took him for an astronomer. However, you know he's not a bad-looking fellow—and a foreigner, a Russian, of course—he took her fancy. Well, at last he invited her to a rendezvous, and a very poetical rendezvous, in a boat on the river. The Frenchwoman agreed; dressed herself in her best and went out with him in a boat. So they spent two hours. How do you think he was occupied all that time? He patted the Frenchwoman on the head, gazed thoughtfully at the sky, and frequently repeated that he felt for her the tenderness of a father. The Frenchwoman went back home in a fury, and she herself told the story to Terlahov afterwards! That's the kind of fellow he is.'

And Pigasov broke into a loud laugh.

'You old cynic!' said Alexandra Pavlovna in a tone of annoyance, 'but I am more and more convinced that even those who attack Rudin cannot find any harm to say of him.'

'No harm? Upon my word! and his perpetual living at other people's expense, his borrowing money.... Mihailo Mihailitch, he borrowed of you too, no doubt, didn't he?'

'Listen, African Semenitch!' began Lezhnyov, and his face assumed a serious expression, 'listen; you know, and my wife knows, that the last time I saw him I felt no special attachment for Rudin, and I even often blamed him. For all that (Lezhnyov filled up the glasses with champagne) this is what I suggest to you now; we have just drunk to the health of my dear brother and his future bride; I propose that you drink now to the health of Dmitri Rudin!'

Alexandra Pavlovna and Pigasov looked in astonishment at Lezhnyov, but Bassistoff sat wide-eyed, blushing and trembling all over with delight.

'I know him well,' continued Lezhnyov, 'I am well aware of his faults. They are the more conspicuous because he himself is not on a small scale.'

'Rudin has character, genius!' cried Bassistoff.

'Genius, very likely he has!' replied Lezhnyov, 'but as for character ... That's just his misfortune, that there's no character in him... But that's not the point.

I want to speak of what is good, of what is rare in him. He has enthusiasm; and believe me, who am a phlegmatic person enough, that is the most precious quality in our times. We have all become insufferably reasonable, indifferent, and slothful; we are asleep and cold, and thanks to any one who will wake us up and warm us! It is high time! Do you remember, Sasha, once when I was talking to you about him, I blamed him for coldness? I was right, and wrong too, then. The coldness is in his blood—that is not his fault—and not in his head. He is not an actor, as I called him, nor a cheat, nor a scoundrel; he lives at other people's expense, not like a swindler, but like a child.... Yes; no doubt he will die somewhere in poverty and want; but are we to throw stones at him for that? He never does anything himself precisely, he has no vital force, no blood; but who has the right to say that he has not been of use? that his words have not scattered good seeds in young hearts, to whom nature has not denied, as she has to him, powers for action, and the faculty of carrying out their own ideas? Indeed, I myself, to begin with, have gained all that from him.... Sasha knows what Rudin did for me in my youth. I also maintained, I recollect, that Rudin's words could not produce an effect on men; but I was speaking then of men like myself, at my present age, of men who have already lived and been broken in by life. One false note in a man's eloquence, and the whole harmony is spoiled for us; but a young man's ear, happily, is not so over-fine, not so trained. If the substance of what he hears seems fine to him, what does he care about the intonation! The intonation he will supply for himself!'

'Bravo, bravo!' cried Bassistoff, 'that is justly spoken! And as regards Rudin's influence, I swear to you, that man not only knows how to move you, he lifts you up, he does not let you stand still, he stirs you to the depths and sets you on fire!'

'You hear?' continued Lezhnyov, turning to Pigasov; 'what further proof do you want? You attack philosophy; speaking of it, you cannot find words contemptuous enough. I myself am not excessively devoted to it, and I know little enough about it; but our principal misfortunes do not come from philosophy! The Russian will never be infected with philosophical hair-splittings and nonsense; he has too much common-sense for that; but we must not let every sincere effort after truth and knowledge be attacked under the name of philosophy. Rudin's misfortune is that he does not understand Russia, and that, certainly, is a great misfortune. Russia can do without every one of us, but not one of us can do without her. Woe to him who thinks he can, and woe twofold to him who actually does do without her! Cosmopolitanism is all twaddle, the cosmopolitan is a nonentity—worse than a nonentity; without nationality is no art, nor truth, nor life, nor anything. You cannot even have an ideal face without individual expression; only a vulgar face can be devoid of it. But I say again, that is not Rudin's fault; it is his fate—a cruel and unhappy fate—for which we cannot blame him. It would take us too far if we tried to trace why Rudins spring up among us. But for what is fine in him, let us be grateful to him. That is pleasanter than being unfair to him, and we have been unfair to him. It's not our business to punish him, and it's not needed; he has punished himself far more cruelly than he deserved. And God grant that unhappiness may have blotted out all the harm there was in him, and left only what was fine! I drink to the health of Rudin! I drink to the comrade of my best years, I drink to youth, to its hopes, its endeavours, its faith, and its honesty, to all that our hearts beat for at twenty; we have known, and shall know, nothing better than that in life.... I drink to that golden time—to the health of Rudin!'

All clinked glasses with Lezhnyov. Bassistoff, in his enthusiasm, almost cracked his glass and drained it off at a draught. Alexandra Pavlovna pressed Lezhnyov's hand.

'Why, Mihailo Mihailitch, I did not suspect you were an orator,' remarked Pigasov; 'it was equal to Mr. Rudin himself; even I was moved by it.'

'I am not at all an orator,' replied Lezhnyov, not without annoyance, 'but to move you, I fancy, would be difficult. But enough of Rudin; let us talk of something else. What of—what's his name—Pandalevsky? is he still living at Darya Mihailovna's?' he concluded, turning to Bassistoff.

'Oh yes, he is still there. She has managed to get him a very profitable place.'

Lezhnyov smiled.

'That's a man who won't die in want, one can count upon that.'

Supper was over. The guests dispersed. When she was left alone with her husband, Alexandra Pavlovna looked smiling into his face.

'How splendid you were this evening, Misha,' she said, stroking his forehead, 'how cleverly and nobly you spoke! But confess, you exaggerated a little in Rudin's praise, as in old days you did in attacking him.'

'I can't let them hit a man when he's down. And in those days I was afraid he was turning your head.'

'No,' replied Alexandra Pavlovna naively, 'he always seemed too learned for me. I was afraid of him, and never knew what to say in his presence. But wasn't Pigasov nasty in his ridicule of him to-day?'

'Pigasov?' responded Lezhnyov. 'That was just why I stood up for Rudin so warmly, because Pigasov was here. He dare to call Rudin a sponge indeed! Why, I consider the part he plays—Pigasov I mean—is a hundred times worse! He has an independent property, and he sneers at every one, and yet see how he fawns upon wealthy or distinguished people! Do you know that

that fellow, who abuses everything and every one with such scorn, and attacks philosophy and women, do you know that when he was in the service, he took bribes and that sort of thing! Ugh! That's what he is!'

'Is it possible?' cried Alexandra Pavlovna, 'I should never have expected that! Misha,' she added, after a short pause, 'I want to ask you——'

'What?'

'What do you think, will my brother be happy with Natalya?'

'How can I tell you?... there's every likelihood of it. She will take the lead... there's no reason to hide the fact between us... she is cleverer than he is; but he's a capital fellow, and loves her with all his soul. What more would you have? You see we love one another and are happy, aren't we?'

Alexandra Pavlovna smiled and pressed his hand.

On the same day on which all that has been described took place in Alexandra Pavlovna's house, in one of the remote districts of Russia, a wretched little covered cart, drawn by three village horses was crawling along the high road in the sultry heat. On the front seat was perched a grizzled peasant in a ragged cloak, with his legs hanging slanting on the shaft; he kept flicking with the reins, which were of cord, and shaking the whip. Inside the cart there was sitting on a shaky portmanteau a tall man in a cap and old dusty cloak. It was Rudin. He sat with bent head, the peak of his cap pulled over his eyes. The jolting of the cart threw him from side to side; but he seemed utterly unconscious, as though he were asleep. At last he drew himself up.

'When are we coming to a station?' he inquired of the peasant sitting in front.

'Just over the hill, little father,' said the peasant, with a still more violent shaking of the reins. 'There's a mile and a half farther to go, not more.... Come! there! look about you.... I'll teach you,' he added in a shrill voice, setting to work to whip the right-hand horse.

'You seem to drive very badly,' observed Rudin; 'we have been crawling along since early morning, and we have not succeeded in getting there yet. You should have sung something.'

'Well, what would you have, little father? The horses, you see yourself, are overdone... and then the heat; and I can't sing. I'm not a coachman.... Hullo, you little sheep!' cried the peasant, suddenly turning to a man coming along in a brown smock and bark shoes downtrodden at heel. 'Get out of the way!'

'You're a nice driver!' muttered the man after him, and stood still. 'You wretched Muscovite,' he added in a voice full of contempt, shook his head and limped away.

'What are you up to?' sang out the peasant at intervals, pulling at the shaft-horse. 'Ah, you devil! Get on!'

The jaded horses dragged themselves at last up to the posting-station. Rudin crept out of the cart, paid the peasant (who did not bow to him, and kept shaking the coins in the palm of his hand a long while—evidently there was too little drink-money) and himself carried the portmanteau into the posting-station.

A friend of mine who has wandered a great deal about Russia in his time made the observation that if the pictures hanging on the walls of a posting-station represent scenes from 'the Prisoner of the Caucasus,' or Russian generals, you may get horses soon; but if the pictures depict the life of the well-known gambler George de Germany, the traveller need not hope to get off quickly; he will have time to admire to the full the hair *à la cockatoo*, the white open waistcoat, and the exceedingly short and narrow trousers of the gambler in his youth, and his exasperated physiognomy, when in his old age he kills his son, waving a chair above him, in a cottage with a narrow staircase. In the room into which Rudin walked precisely these pictures were hanging out of 'Thirty Years, or the Life of a Gambler.' In response to his call the superintendent appeared, who had just waked up (by the way, did any one ever see a superintendent who had not just been asleep?), and without even waiting for Rudin's question, informed him in a sleepy voice that there were no horses.

'How can you say there are no horses,' said Rudin, 'when you don't even know where I am going? I came here with village horses.'

'We have no horses for anywhere,' answered the superintendent. 'But where are you going?'

'To Sk——.'

'We have no horses,' repeated the superintendent, and he went away.

Rudin, vexed, went up to the window and threw his cap on the table. He was not much changed, but had grown rather yellow in the last two years; silver threads shone here and there in his curls, and his eyes, still magnificent, seemed somehow dimmed, fine lines, the traces of bitter and disquieting emotions, lay about his lips and on his temples. His clothes were shabby and old, and he had no linen visible anywhere. His best days were clearly over: as the gardeners say, he had gone to seed.

He began reading the inscriptions on the walls—the ordinary distraction of weary travellers; suddenly the door creaked and the superintendent came in.

'There are no horses for Sk——, and there won't be any for a long time,' he said, 'but here are some ready to go to V——.'

'To V——?' said Rudin. 'Why, that's not on my road at all. I am going to Penza, and V—— lies, I think, in the direction of Tamboff.'

'What of that? you can get there from Tamboff, and from V—— you won't be at all out of your road.'

Rudin thought a moment.

'Well, all right,' he said at last, 'tell them to put the horses to. It is the same to me; I will go to Tamboff.'

The horses were soon ready. Rudin carried his own portmanteau, climbed into the cart, and took his seat, his head hanging as before. There was something helpless and pathetically submissive in his bent figure.... And the three horses went off at a slow trot.

EPILOGUE

Some years had passed by.

It was a cold autumn day. A travelling carriage drew up at the steps of the principal hotel of the government town of C——; a gentleman yawning and stretching stepped out of it. He was not elderly, but had had time to acquire that fulness of figure which habitually commands respect. He went up the staircase to the second story, and stopped at the entrance to a wide corridor. Seeing no one before him he called out in a loud voice asking for a room. A door creaked somewhere, and a long waiter jumped up from behind a low screen, and came forward with a quick flank movement, an apparition of a glossy back and tucked-up sleeves in the half-dark corridor. The traveller went into the room and at once throwing off his cloak and scarf, sat down on the sofa, and with his fists propped on his knees, he first looked round as though he were hardly awake yet, and then gave the order to send up his servant. The hotel waiter made a bow and disappeared. The traveller was no other than Lezhnyov. He had come from the country to C—— about some conscription business.

Lezhnyov's servant, a curly-headed, rosy-cheeked youth in a grey cloak, with a blue sash round the waist, and soft felt shoes, came into the room.

'Well, my boy, here we are,' Lezhnyov said, 'and you were afraid all the while that a wheel would come off.'

'We are here,' replied the boy, trying to smile above the high collar of his cloak, 'but the reason why the wheel did not come off——'

'Is there no one in here?' sounded a voice in the corridor.

Lezhnyov started and listened.

'Eh? who is there?' repeated the voice.

Lezhnyov got up, walked to the door, and quickly threw it open.

Before him stood a tall man, bent and almost completely grey, in an old frieze coat with bronze buttons.

'Rudin!' he cried in an excited voice.

Rudin turned round. He could not distinguish Lezhnyov's features, as he stood with his back to the light, and he looked at him in bewilderment.

'You don't know me?' said Lezhnyov.

'Mihailo Mihailitch!' cried Rudin, and held out his hand, but drew it back again in confusion. Lezhnyov made haste to snatch it in both of his.

'Come, come in!' he said to Rudin, and drew him into the room.

'How you have changed!' exclaimed Lezhnyov after a brief silence, involuntarily dropping his voice.

'Yes, they say so!' replied Rudin, his eyes straying about the room. 'The years... and you not much. How is Alexandra—your wife?'

'She is very well, thank you. But what fate brought you here?'

'It is too long a story. Strictly speaking, I came here by chance. I was looking for a friend. But I am very glad...'

'Where are you going to dine?'

'Oh, I don't know. At some restaurant. I must go away from here to-day.'

'You must.'

Rudin smiled significantly.

'Yes, I must. They are sending me off to my own place, to my home.'

'Dine with me.'

Rudin for the first time looked Lezhnyov straight in the face.

'You invite me to dine with you?' he said.

'Yes, Rudin, for the sake of old times and old comradeship. Will you? I did not expect to meet you, and God only knows when we shall see each other again. I cannot part from you like this!'

'Very well, I agree!'

Lezhnyov pressed Rudin's hand, and calling his servant, ordered dinner, and told him to have a bottle of champagne put in ice.

In the course of dinner, Lezhnyov and Rudin, as though by agreement, kept talking of their student days, recalling many things and many friends—dead and living. At first Rudin spoke with little interest, but when he had drunk a few glasses of wine his blood grew warmer. At last the waiter took away the last dish, Lezhnyov got up, closed the door, and coming back to the table, sat down facing Rudin, and quietly rested his chin on his hands.

'Now, then,' he began, 'tell me all that has happened to you since I saw you last.'

Rudin looked at Lezhnyov.

'Good God!' thought Lezhnyov, 'how he has changed, poor fellow!'

Rudin's features had undergone little change since we saw him last at the posting-station, though approaching old age had had time to set its mark upon them; but their expression had become different. His eyes had a changed look; his whole being, his movements, which were at one time slow, at another abrupt and disconnected, his crushed, benumbed manner of speaking, all showed an utter exhaustion, a quiet and secret dejection, very different from the half-assumed melancholy which he had affected once, as it is generally affected by youth, when full of hopes and confident vanity.

'Tell you all that has happened to me?' he said; 'I could not tell you all, and it is not worth while. I am worn out; I have wandered far—in spirit as well as in flesh. What friends I have made—good God! How many things, how many men I have lost faith in! Yes, how many!' repeated Rudin, noticing that Lezhnyov was looking in his face with a kind of special sympathy. 'How many times have my own words grown hateful to me! I don't mean now on my own lips, but on the lips of those who had adopted my opinions! How many times have I passed from the petulance of a child to the dull insensibility of a horse who does not lash his tail when the whip cuts him!... How many times I have been happy and hopeful, and have made enemies and humbled myself for nothing! How many times I have taken flight like an eagle—and returned crawling like a snail whose shell has been crushed!... Where have I not been! What roads have I not travelled!... And the roads are often dirty,' added Rudin, slightly turning away. 'You know ...' he was continuing.... 'Listen,' interrupted Lezhnyov. 'We used once to say "Dmitri and Mihail" to one another. Let us revive the old habit,... will you? Let us drink to those days!'

Rudin started and drew himself up a little, and there was a gleam in his eyes of something no word can express.

'Let us drink to them,' he said. 'I thank you, brother, we will drink to them!'

Lezhnyov and Rudin drained their glasses.

'You know, Mihail,' Rudin began again with a smile and a stress on the name, 'there is a worm in me which gnaws and worries me and never lets me be at peace till the end. It brings me into collision with people,—at first they fall under my influence, but afterwards...'

Rudin waved his hand in the air.

'Since I parted from you, Mihail, I have seen much, have experienced many changes.... I have begun life, have started on something new twenty times—and here—you see!'

'You had no stability,' said Lezhnyov, as though to himself.

'As you say, I had no stability. I never was able to construct anything; and it's a difficult thing, brother, to construct when one has to create the very ground under one's feet, to make one's own foundation for one's self! All my adventures—that is, speaking accurately, all my failures, I will not describe. I will tell of two or three incidents—those incidents of my life when it seemed as if success were smiling on me, or rather when I began to hope for success—which is not altogether the same thing...'

Rudin pushed back his grey and already sparse locks with the same gesture which he used once to toss back his thick, dark curls.

'Well, I will tell you, Mihail,' he began. 'In Moscow I came across a rather strange man. He was very wealthy and was the owner of extensive estates. His chief and only passion was love of science, universal science. I have never yet been able to arrive at how this passion arose in him! It fitted him about as well as a saddle on a cow. He managed with difficulty to maintain himself at his mental elevation, he was almost without the power of speech, he only rolled his eyes with expression and shook his head significantly. I never met, brother, a poorer and less gifted nature than his.... In the Smolensk province there are places like that—nothing but sand and a few tufts of grass which no animal can eat. Nothing succeeded in his hands; everything seemed to slip away from him; but he was still mad on making everything plain complicated. If it had depended on his arrangements, his people would have eaten standing on their heads. He worked, and wrote, and read indefatigably. He devoted himself to science with a kind of stubborn perseverance, a terrible patience; his vanity was immense, and he had a will of iron. He lived alone, and had the reputation of an eccentric. I made friends with him... and he liked me. I quickly, I must own, saw through him; but his zeal attracted me. Besides, he was the master of such resources; so much good might be done, so much real usefulness through him.... I was installed in his house and went with him to the country. My plans, brother, were on a vast scale; I dreamed of various reforms, innovations...'

'Just as at the Lasunsky's, do you remember, Dmitri?' responded Lezhnyov, with an indulgent smile.

'Ah, but then I knew in my heart that nothing would come of my words; but this time... an altogether different field of activity lay open before me.... I took with me books on agriculture... to tell the truth, I did not read one of them through.... Well, I set to work. At first it did not progress as I had expected; but afterwards it did get on in a way. My new friend looked on and said nothing; he did not interfere with me, at least not to any noticeable extent. He accepted my suggestions, and carried them out, but with a stubborn sullenness, a secret want of faith; and he bent everything his own way. He prized extremely every idea of his own. He got to it with difficulty, like a ladybird on a blade of grass, and he would sit and sit upon it, as though pluming his wings and getting ready for a flight, and suddenly he would fall off and begin crawling again.... Don't be surprised at these comparisons; at that time they were always crowding on my imagination. So I struggled on there for two years. The work did not progress much in spite of all my efforts. I began to be tired of it, my friend bored me; I had come to sneer at him, and he stifled me like a featherbed; his want of faith had changed into a dumb resentment; a feeling of hostility had laid hold of both of us; we could scarcely now speak of anything; he quietly but incessantly tried to show me that he was not under my influence; my arrangements were either set aside or altogether transformed. I realised, at last, that I was playing the part of a toady in the noble landowner's house by providing him with intellectual amusement. It was very bitter to me to have wasted my time and strength for nothing, most bitter to feel that I had again and again been deceived in my expectations. I knew very well what I was losing if I went away; but I could not control myself, and one day after a painful and revolting scene of which I was a witness, and which showed my friend in a most disadvantageous light, I quarrelled with him finally, went away, and threw up this newfangled pedant, made of a queer compound of our native flour kneaded up with German treacle.'

'That is, you threw up your daily bread, Dmitri,' said Lezhnyov, laying both hands on Rudin's shoulders.

'Yes, and again I was turned adrift, empty-handed and penniless, to fly whither I listed. Ah! let us drink!'

'To your health!' said Lezhnyov, getting up and kissing Rudin on the forehead. 'To your health and to the memory of Pokorsky. He, too, knew how to be poor.'

'Well, that was number one of my adventures,' began Rudin, after a short pause. 'Shall I go on?'

'Go on, please.'

'Ah! I have no wish for talking. I am tired of talking, brother.... However, so be it. After knocking about in various parts—by the way, I might tell you how I became the secretary of a benevolent dignitary, and what came of that; but that would take me too long.... After knocking about in various parts, I resolved to become at last—don't smile, please—a practical business man. The opportunity came in this way. I became friendly with—he was much talked of at one time—a man called Kurbyev.'

'Oh, I never heard of him. But, really, Dmitri, with your intelligence, how was it you did not suspect that to be a business man was not the business for you?'

'I know, brother, that it was not; but, then, what is the business for me? But if you had seen Kurbyev! Do not, pray, fancy him as some empty-headed chatterer. They say I was eloquent once. I was simply nothing beside him. He was a man of wonderful learning and knowledge,—an intellect, brother, a creative intellect, for business and commercial enterprises. His brain seemed seething with the boldest, the most unexpected schemes. I joined him and we decided to turn our powers to a work of public utility.'

'What was it, may I know?'

Rudin dropped his eyes.

'You will laugh at it, Mihail.'

'Why should I? No, I will not laugh.'

'We resolved to make a river in the K—— province fit for navigation,' said Rudin with an embarrassed smile.

'Really! This Kurbyev was a capitalist, then?'

'He was poorer than I,' responded Rudin, and his grey head sank on his breast.

Lezhnyov began to laugh, but he stopped suddenly and took Rudin by the hand.

'Pardon me, brother, I beg,' he said, 'but I did not expect that. Well, so I suppose your enterprise did not get further than paper?'

'Not so. A beginning was made. We hired workmen, and set to work. But then we were met by various obstacles. In the first place the millowners would not meet us favourably at all; and more than that, we could not turn the water out of its course without machinery, and we had not money enough for machinery. For six months we lived in mud huts. Kurbyev lived on dry bread, and I, too, had not much to eat. However, I don't complain of that; the scenery there is something magnificent. We struggled and struggled on, appealing to merchants, writing letters and circulars. It ended in my spending my last farthing on the project.'

'Well!' observed Lezhnyov, 'I imagine to spend your last farthing, Dmitri, was not a difficult matter?'

'It was not difficult, certainly.'

Rudin looked out of the window.

'But the project really was not a bad one, and it might have been of immense service.'

'And where did Kurbyev go to?' asked Lezhnyov.

'Oh, he is now in Siberia, he has become a gold-digger. And you will see he will make himself a position; he will get on.'

'Perhaps; but then you will not be likely to make a position for yourself, it seems.'

'Well, that can't be helped! But I know I was always a frivolous creature in your eyes.'

'Hush, brother; there was a time, certainly, when I saw your weak side; but now, believe me, I have learnt to value you. You will not make yourself a position. And I love you, Dmitri, for that, indeed I do!'

Rudin smiled faintly.

'Truly?'

'I respect you for it!' repeated Lezhnyov. 'Do you understand me?'

Both were silent for a little.

'Well, shall I proceed to number three?' asked Rudin.

'Please do.'

'Very well. The third and last. I have only now got clear of number three. But am I not boring you, Mihail?'

'Go on, go on.'

'Well,' began Rudin, 'once the idea occurred to me at some leisure moment— I always had plenty of leisure moments—the idea occurred to me; I have knowledge enough, my intentions are good. I suppose even you will not deny me good intentions?'

'I should think not!'

'In all other directions I had failed more or less... why should I not become an instructor, or speaking simply a teacher... rather than waste my life?'

Rudin stopped and sighed.

'Rather than waste my life, would it not be better to try to pass on to others what I know; perhaps they may extract at least some use from my knowledge. My abilities are above the ordinary anyway, I am a master of language. So I resolved to devote myself to this new work. I had difficulty in obtaining a post; I did not want to give private lessons; there was nothing I could do in the lower schools. At last I succeeded in getting an appointment as professor in the gymnasium here.'

'As professor of what?' asked Lezhnyov.

'Professor of literature. I can tell you I never started on any work with such zest as I did on this. The thought of producing an effect upon the young inspired me. I spent three weeks over the composition of my opening lecture.'

'Have you got it, Dmitri?' interrupted Lezhnyov.

'No! I lost it somewhere. It went off fairly well, and was liked. I can see now the faces of my listeners—good young faces, with an expression of pure-souled attention and sympathy, and even of amazement. I mounted the platform and read my lecture in a fever; I thought it would fill more than an hour, but I had finished it in twenty minutes. The inspector was sitting there—a dry old man in silver spectacles and a short wig—he sometimes turned his head in my direction. When I had finished, he jumped up from his seat and said to me, "Good, but rather over their heads, obscure, and too little said about the subject." But the pupils followed me with appreciation in their looks—indeed they did. Ah, that is how youth is so precious! I gave a second written lecture, and a third. After that I began to lecture extempore.'

'And you had success?' asked Lezhnyov.

'I had a great success. I gave my audience all that was in my soul. Among them were two or three really remarkable boys; the rest did not understand me much. I must confess though that even those who did understand me sometimes embarrassed me by their questions. But I did not lose heart. They all loved me; I gave them all full marks in examinations. But then an intrigue was started against me—or no! it was not an intrigue at all; it simply was, that I was not in my proper place. I was a hindrance to the others, and they were a hindrance to me. I lectured to the gymnasium pupils in a way lectures are not given every day, even to students; they carried away very little from my lectures.... I myself did not know the facts enough. Besides, I was not satisfied with the limited sphere assigned to me—you know that is always my weakness. I wanted radical reforms, and I swear to you that these reforms were both sensible and easy to carry out. I hoped to carry them through the director, a good and honest man, over whom I had at first some influence. His wife aided me. I have not, brother, met many women like her in my life. She was about forty; but she believed in goodness, and loved everything fine with the enthusiasm of a girl of fifteen, and was not afraid to give utterance to her convictions before any one whatever. I shall never forget her generous enthusiasm and goodness. By her advice I drew up a plan.... But then my influence was undermined, I was misrepresented to her. My chief enemy was the professor of mathematics, a little sour, bilious man who believed in nothing, a character like Pigasov, but far more able than he was.... By the way, how is Pigasov, is he living?'

'Oh, yes; and only fancy, he is married to a peasant woman, who, they say, beats him.'

'Serve him right! And Natalya Alexyevna—is she well?'

'Yes.'

'Is she happy?'

'Yes.'

Rudin was silent for a little.

'What was I talking about?... Oh yes! about the professor of mathematics. He perfectly hated me; he compared my lectures to fireworks, pounced upon every expression of mine that was not altogether clear, once even put me to confusion over some monument of the sixteenth century.... But the most important thing was, he suspected my intentions; my last soap-bubble struck on him as on a spike, and burst. The inspector, whom I had not got on with from the first, set the director against me. A scene followed. I was not ready to give in; I got hot; the matter came to the knowledge of the authorities; I was forced to resign. I did not stop there; I wanted to prove that they could not treat me like that.... But they could treat me as they liked.... Now I am forced to leave the town.'

A silence followed. Both the friends sat with bowed heads.

Rudin was the first to speak.

'Yes, brother,' he began, 'I can say now, in the words of Koltsov, "Thou hast led me astray, my youth, till there is nowhere I can turn my steps."... And yet can it be that I was fit for nothing, that for me there was, as it were, no work on earth to do? I have often put myself this question, and, however much I tried to humble myself in my own eyes, I could not but feel the existence of faculties within me which are not given to every one! Why have these faculties remained fruitless? And let me say more; you know, when I was with you abroad, Mihail, I was conceited and full of erroneous ideas.... Certainly I did not then realise clearly what I wanted; I lived upon words, and believed in phantoms. But now, I swear to you, I could speak out before all men every desire I feel. I have absolutely nothing to hide; I am absolutely, in the fullest meaning of the word, a well-intentioned man. I am humble, I am ready to adapt myself to circumstances; I want little; I want to do the good that lies nearest, to be even a little use. But no! I never succeed. What does it mean? What hinders me from living and working like others?... I am only dreaming of it now. But no sooner do I get into any definite position when fate throws the dice from me. I have come to dread it—my destiny.... Why is it so? Explain this enigma to me!'

'An enigma!' repeated Lezhnyov. 'Yes, that's true; you have always been an enigma for me. Even in our young days, when, after some trifling prank, you would suddenly speak as though you were pierced to the heart, and then you would begin again... well you know what I mean... even then I did not understand. That is why I grew apart from you.... You have so much power, such unwearying striving after the ideal.'

'Words, all words! There was nothing done!' Rudin broke in.

'Nothing done! What is there to do?'

'What is there to do! To keep an old blind woman and all her family by one's work, as, do you remember, Mihail, Pryazhentsov did... That's doing something.'

'Yes, but a good word—is also something done.'

Rudin looked at Lezhnyov without speaking and faintly shook his head.

Lezhnyov wanted to say something, and he passed his hand over his face.

'And so you are going to your country place?' he asked at last.

'Yes.'

'There you have some property left?'

'Something is left me there. Two souls and a half. It is a corner to die in. You are thinking perhaps at this moment: "Even now he cannot do without fine words!" Words indeed have been my ruin; they have consumed me, and to the end I cannot be free of them. But what I have said was not mere words. These white hairs, brother, these wrinkles, these ragged elbows—they are not mere words. You have always been hard on me, Mihail, and you were right; but now is not a time to be hard, when all is over, when there's no oil left in the lamp, and the lamp itself is broken, and the wick is just smouldering out. Death, brother, should reconcile at last...'

Lezhnyov jumped up.

'Rudin!' he cried, 'why do you speak like that to me? How have I deserved it from you? Am I such a judge, and what kind of a man should I be, if at the sight of your hollow cheeks and wrinkles, "mere words" could occur to my mind? Do you want to know what I think of you, Dmitri? Well! I think: here is a man—with his abilities, what might he not have attained to, what worldly advantages might he not have possessed by now, if he had liked!... and I meet him hungry and homeless....'

'I rouse your compassion,' Rudin murmured in a choked voice.

'No, you are wrong. You inspire respect in me—that is what I feel. Who prevented you from spending year after year at that landowner's, who was your friend, and who would, I am fully persuaded, have made provision for you, if you had only been willing to humour him? Why could you not live harmoniously at the gymnasium, why have you—strange man!—with whatever ideas you have entered upon an undertaking, infallibly every time ended by sacrificing your personal interests, ever refusing to take root in any but good ground, however profitable it might be?'

'I was born a rolling stone,' Rudin said, with a weary smile. 'I cannot stop myself.'

'That is true; but you cannot stop, not because there is a worm gnawing you, as you said to me at first.... It is not a worm, not the spirit of idle restlessness—it is the fire of the love of truth that burns in you, and clearly, in spite of your failings; it burns in you more hotly than in many who do not consider themselves egoists and dare to call you a humbug perhaps. I, for one, in your place should long ago have succeeded in silencing that worm in me, and should have given in to everything; and you have not even been embittered by it, Dmitri. You are ready, I am sure, to-day, to set to some new work again like a boy.'

'No, brother, I am tired now,' said Rudin. 'I have had enough.'

'Tired! Any other man would have been dead long ago. You say that death reconciles; but does not life, don't you think, reconcile? A man who has lived and has not grown tolerant towards others does not deserve to meet with tolerance himself. And who can say he does not need tolerance? You have done what you could, Dmitri... you have struggled so long as you could... what more? Our paths lay apart,'...

'You were utterly different from me,' Rudin put in with a sigh.

'Our paths lay apart,' continued Lezhnyov, 'perhaps exactly because, thanks to my position, my cool blood, and other fortunate circumstances, nothing hindered me from being a stay-at-home, and remaining a spectator with folded hands; but you had to go out into the world, to turn up your shirt-sleeves, to toil and labour. Our paths lay apart—but see how near one another we are. We speak almost the same language, with half a hint we understand one another, we grew up on the same ideas. There is little left us now, brother; we are the last of the Mohicans! We might differ and even quarrel in old days, when so much life still remained before us; but now, when the ranks are thinned about us, when the younger generation is coming upon us with other aims than ours, we ought to keep close to one another! Let us clink glasses, Dmitri, and sing as of old, *Gaudeamus igitur!*'

The friends clinked their glasses, and sang the old student song in strained voices, all out of tune, in the true Russian style.

'So you are going now to your country place,' Lezhnyov began again. 'I don't think you will stay there long, and I cannot imagine where and how you will end.... But remember, whatever happens to you, you have always a place, a nest where you can hide yourself. That is my home,—do you hear, old fellow? Thought, too, has its veterans; they, too, ought to have their home.'

Rudin got up.

'Thanks, brother,' he said, 'thanks! I will not forget this in you. Only I do not deserve a home. I have wasted my life, and have not served thought, as I ought.'

'Hush!' said Lezhnyov. 'Every man remains what Nature has made him, and one cannot ask more of him! You have called yourself the Wandering Jew.... But how do you know,—perhaps it was right for you to be ever wandering, perhaps in that way you are fulfilling a higher calling than you know; popular wisdom says truly that we are all in God's hands. You are going, Dmitri,' continued Lezhnyov, seeing that Rudin was taking his hat 'You will not stop the night?'

'Yes, I am going! Good-bye. Thanks.... I shall come to a bad end.'

'God only knows.... You are resolved to go?'

'Yes, I am going. Good-bye. Do not remember evil against me.'

'Well, do not remember evil against me either,—and don't forget what I said to you. Good-bye.'...

The friends embraced one another. Rudin went quickly away.

Lezhnyov walked up and down the room a long while, stopped before the window thinking, and murmured half aloud, 'Poor fellow!' Then sitting down to the table, he began to write a letter to his wife.

But outside a wind had risen, and was howling with ill-omened moans, and wrathfully shaking the rattling window-panes. The long autumn night came on. Well for the man on such a night who sits under the shelter of home, who has a warm corner in safety.... And the Lord help all homeless wanderers!

On a sultry afternoon on the 26th of July in 1848 in Paris, when the Revolution of the *ateliers nationaux* had already been almost suppressed, a line battalion was taking a barricade in one of the narrow alleys of the Faubourg St Antoine. A few gunshots had already broken it; its surviving defenders abandoned it, and were only thinking of their own safety, when suddenly on the very top of the barricade, on the frame of an overturned omnibus, appeared a tall man in an old overcoat, with a red sash, and a straw hat on his grey dishevelled hair. In one hand he held a red flag, in the other a blunt curved sabre, and as he scrambled up, he shouted something in a shrill strained voice, waving his flag and sabre. A Vincennes tirailleur took aim at him—fired. The tall man dropped the flag—and like a sack he toppled over face downwards, as though he were falling at some one's feet. The bullet had passed through his heart.

'*Tiens*!' said one of the escaping revolutionists to another, '*on vient de tuer le Polonais*!'

'*Bigre*!' answered the other, and both ran into the cellar of a house, the shutters of which were all closed, and its wall streaked with traces of powder and shot.

This 'Polonais' was Dmitri Rudin.

THE END.